BOWDRIE—TOUGH ENOUGH?

"Jest set right still, Ranger. An' keep both hands on the pommel."

Chick Bowdrie swore softly. Too late now, he saw the two rifle barrels and they were pointed at him. It would be madness to move now. At that distance they could not miss.

Shad Tucker came out of the brush. Behind him was Buckeye Thomas. Thomas bared his yellow teeth. "The great Chick Bowdrie! Wal, Mr. Ranger, I reckon you got to be taught. I reckon so."

Tucker gestured at the maze of canyons and rough country. "This here's mine! You Rangers ain't needed. We'll just sort of make an example of you an' leave what's left for Rangers to find so they'll know what's comin' to 'em if they come into my country."

Tucker reached up and flipped Bowdrie's guns from their holsters, then, grabbing him by the shirtfront, he jerked him from the saddle and threw a wicked punch to his belly.

"How d'you like it, Ranger? You think you're tough, huh? Well, we'll see."

Bantam Books by Louis L'Amour
Ask your bookseller for the books you have missed.

BOWDRIE'S LAW

Louis L'Amour

BANTAM BOOKS
NEW YORK · TORONTO · LONDON · SYDNEY · AUCKLAND

To
Jim Messersmith,
Larry Messersmith,
Bob Christy,
Jim Gillam,
Cliff Bothe,
Tre Bothe,
Frank Jarnagan,
James Myers, and
Sonny Martinez
who restored my log cabin.

BOWDRIE'S LAW
A Bantam Book / December 1984

*Photograph of Louis L'Amour by John Hamilton—
Globe Photos, Inc.*

ISBN 0-553-24550-3

Published simultaneously in the United States and Canada

*Bantam Books are published by Bantam Books, Inc. Its trademark,
consisting of the words "Bantam Books" and the portrayal of a rooster, is
Registered in U.S. Patent and Trademark Office and in other countries.
Marca Registrada. Bantam Books, Inc., 666 Fifth Avenue, New York,
New York 10103.*

PRINTED IN THE UNITED STATES OF AMERICA

OPM   17 16 15 14 13 12 11 10

CONTENTS

Foreword

Was the West really wild? Much depends on one's definition, as well as one's viewpoint. There were areas of comparative quiet, and much of the "in town" violence occurred in the saloons or the red-light districts. Church services, social affairs among the town's outstanding citizens, or quiet evenings at home were rarely disturbed by distant gunshots.

On the other hand, in the period between 1865 and 1892 there were 823 battles between the Indians and the Army. That says nothing about raids upon ranches, settlers' homes, or the various conflicts between private citizens and the Indians. Fights such as the one told elsewhere in this book, "The Buffalo Wallow Fight," would not be listed by the Army. It was simply too small to be considered a battle.

Neill Wilson, in his excellent book *Treasure Express*, lists a series of Wells Fargo holdups that took place in one period of 14 years. In that period there were 313 robberies of stages and 34 more were attempted. Of the robbers, 16 were killed, 7 hanged by irate citizens, and 240 convicted.

Wells Fargo was only one express company, and these were only horse-drawn stages. The above listing does not include train robberies and, of course, has nothing to say of robberies of other kinds at other places. One can safely say there was considerable criminal activity at the time.

Cattle and sheep wars were numerous, and there were feuds between families or factions, some of which lasted for years and involved pitched battles as well as numerous gunfights. In the case of the family feuds, there were some outright murders.

The Sutton-Taylor Feud, the Mason County War, the Lee-Peacock affair, the Horrell-Higgins fight, the Lincoln County War, and the Graham-Tewksbury fight in the Tonto Basin of Arizona were only a few of those that actually took place, and most of the writing on the subject centers around the cattle drive period, the Texas-to-Kansas route and the action at either end. Attention is also given to Tombstone, and Deadwood gets a quick glance because of the killing there of James Butler Hickok.

The Johnson County War of 1892 was another such, although most of the killings took place before the Invaders arrived to attack Nate Champion on the KC Ranch. The movie *Heaven's Gate* was based on this conflict, and in it the ranchers are shown riding rough-shod over a bunch of Russian immigrants. Nothing could be less true. This movie is now circulating abroad, presenting a portrayal of events that has nothing to do with the truth. No Russians were involved. That is pure invention. The participants were homesteaders and ranchers, most of whom were Anglo-Saxon, Scotch or Irish on both sides. In the motion picture Nate Champion is portrayed as a gunman riding for the big cattlemen. As a matter of fact, he was the one they most wished to kill!

Of course, the West was wild. Much of it was wide open country (and much still is) where a man's life often depended on his horse. There were vast plains, then mountains, and after that desert and more mountains. It was a place where a man might lose himself, and some did. These men, however, were rarely outlaws. The latter were, despite what many may believe, usually gregarious. They did not want money to buy food, they wanted it for whiskey, women, and gambling, and this necessitated being where people were.

Very few eluded the law for long, for the money was of no use while they hid out in the hills. They had to come to town, and the towns were so small, nearly everybody knew what everybody else was doing and strangers were noticed. Moreover, the robbers and the robbed, as well as the lawmen, went often to the same saloons, where voices could be remembered, clothing recognized, and questions might be asked.

In the earliest years men often settled disputes with guns, and as long as the fight had some semblance of an even break the law paid small attention. When a man carried a pistol, it was expected he could use it, and if he could not or was unwilling to, he was better off unarmed.

As the West became more organized the law tightened its grip and gunplay was no longer tolerated as it once had been. Shootings in town became rare, except when bandits attempted a robbery, which gave the local boys a chance to unlimber their artillery and get into action.

It is an interesting fact that those gunfighters usually credited with being the most dangerous were on the side of the law. John Wesley Hardin was for a time an outlaw because of his killings, but he was a cattle drover, occasionally a gambler; he was never a thief. Hickok, Tilghman, Masterson, Milton, the Earps, Stoudenmire, Slaughter, Gillette, McDonald, all wore the badge.

The men who rode the western trail were individuals, men accustomed to handling their own problems, and most of them had grown up using firearms. Many were veterans of the Civil and Indian wars; many were from the border states, those states that bordered on the wild country. They were often half-wild themselves, states such as Missouri, Arkansas, Iowa, Illinois, Tennessee, and Kentucky. These men were not trouble hunters, but when it came to them, they knew what to do.

It has been estimated that 20,000 men were killed in various pistol arbitrations in the West. I believe that figure is too large, but not by very much.

McNelly Knows A Ranger

He rode up to Miller's Crossing just after sundown and stopped at the stage station. Stepping down from the saddle he stood for a moment, taking in the street, the storefronts, and the lighted saloons.

Turning abruptly he crossed the boardwalk into a saloon. The bartender looked up, swallowed hard, and then turned quickly to polishing the back bar. The loafers at the tables glanced at each other, and one picked up a deck of cards and began riffling them nervously.

Bowdrie's question warned them they had not been mistaken. "Where'll I find Noah Whipple?"

The bartender's Adam's apple bobbed. "He—they—they shot him."

"Killed?"

Bowdrie's eyes were cold. The bartender swallowed again and shifted his feet uncomfortably, staring in fascination at the man with the dimplelike scar under the cheekbone below his right eye.

"It was Aaron Fobes done it, Mr. Bowdrie. He's one o' the Ballards."

Bowdrie stood silent, waiting.

"About two this afternoon. They come ridin' in, five of them. Four got down an' come in here. The other'n stayed by the horses. They looked to be a purty salty outfit. They'd been ridin' hard by the look of the horses.

"They took a quick look around when they come in and paid no attention after. They seen everything with that first look. We all knew who they was, even without that holdup over at Benton where they killed the cashier. Everybody knows the Ballards are ridin' again and there ain't two gangs alike.

"The tall one I spotted right off. Had a blaze of white hair over his temple. That would be Clyde Ballard. He's a known man in Texas, from the Rio Grande to the Cimarron.

"The tall gent with the towhead, that would be Cousin Northup, and the slim, dark-faced youngster was Tom Ballard. The other two was Aaron Fobes and Luther Doyle."

"You seem to know them pretty well," Bowdrie commented. "Tell me more."

"Noah, he come in here three or four minutes before the Ballards got here. You maybe know about Noah. He was a good man, no trouble to anybody, but Noah was a talker. He hadn't paid no attention when the Ballards came in, just a glance and he went on talkin'.

" 'Feller come through last night an' said the Ballards was ridin' again. Used to know that Fobes up in the Nation.' We tried to catch his eye but there was no stoppin' him. 'That Fobes,' he says, 'never was no account. Poison mean, he was, even then.

" 'Time's a-comin' when they won't let thieves like that ride around the country robbin' decent people.' Noah was just talkin' like he always done but Fobes was right there to hear him. Fobes tapped him on the shoulder. 'You talk too much, stranger,' he said, speakin' kind of low and mean."

Chick Bowdrie listened, seeing the scene all too clearly, and the inevitable ending. That was Noah, all right, always talking, meaning no harm to anybody, a decent, hardworking man with a family. At least, there was Joanie. Thinking of her his face tightened and he felt empty and kind of sick inside.

"Fobes, he said to Noah that maybe he'd like to stop the Ballards from ridin' the country? Maybe he'd like to try stoppin' them himself?

"Well, you know Noah. He might have been a talker but he was no coward. 'Maybe I would,' Whipple says. 'This country should be made safe for honest people.'

"Clyde Ballard put in then. 'Forget it, Aaron. He didn't know what he was sayin'. Let's ride.' Tom Ballard, he started for the door, Northup followin'. Noah Whipple thought it was all over, an' he dropped his hand.

"He never should have done it, but Noah was a habity man. He was reachin' for a chaw. He chawed tobacco, an' especially when he was nervous or bothered by somethin'. He reached for his tobacco an' Aaron shot him.

"It happened so quick nobody had time to move or speak. Clyde Ballard swore, and then they made a run for their horses and rode off. Noah was dead on the floor, drilled right through the heart, and him not wearin' no gun."

Chick was silent. He looked at the rye whiskey in his glass and thought of Joanie. Only a few months before he had ridden up to their ranch as close to death as a man is apt to get, with three bullet holes in him and having lost a great deal of blood.

Joanie had helped him from his horse and she and Noah had gotten him inside, then nursed him back to health. When able to ride again he had started helping around the ranch. He had not yet become a Ranger and the Whipples needed help. There was only Noah, his wife, and Joanie. They had two old cowhands but they were not much help with the rough stock.

Ranching folks weren't inclined to ask questions of those who drifted around the country. You took a man for what he was and gave him the benefit of the doubt as long as he did his share and shaped up right. Hard-faced young men wearing two tied-down guns weren't seen around very much, even in that country.

Names didn't count for much and both Whipple and Joanie knew that any man wearing two guns was either a man who needed them or a plain damned fool.

He never told them his name. To them he was simply Chick. Noah and his wife treated him like a son, and Joanie like a brother, most of the time.

It had taken him a while to regain his strength but as soon as he was able to get around he started helping, and he had always been a first-rate cowhand.

Bowdrie walked outside the saloon and stood there on the street. He knew what he had to do, and nobody had to ask his intentions. It was the kind of a country where if you worked with a man and ate his bread, you bought some of his troubles, too. The townspeople remembered him as a young cowhand who had worked for Noah, and they also knew he had come into the country in a dying condition from bullet wounds. Why or how he obtained the wounds, nobody ever asked, although curiosity was a festering thing.

He tightened his cinch, stepped back into the leather, and rode out of town.

Two days later Bowdrie rode back to Miller's Crossing. Folks working around town saw him ride in and they noted the brightness of the new Winchester he was carrying.

Bill Anniston, who ranched a small spread not far from the Whipples', was standing on the steps of the stage station when Bowdrie rode up. He had ridden with Bill on a roundup when the two outfits were gathering cattle.

"Bill, I'd take it as a favor if you'd ride over to the Whipples' an' see if they're all right." Bowdrie paused, rubbing the neck of the hammerhead roan. "I joined up with McNelly. I'm ridin' with the Rangers now."

"You goin' after the Ballards?"

"Time somebody did. McNelly said he'd send some

men as soon as they finished what they were doin', but I told him I didn't figure I'd need no help."

As he rode away Bowdrie heard someone say, "I wonder why McNelly would take on a kid like that?"

Bill Anniston replied, "McNelly doesn't make mistakes. He knew what he was doing. Believe me, I've ridden with that boy and he's brush-wise and mountain-smart. He's no flat country yearlin'!"

Bowdrie rode south into the rough country. The wicked-looking hammerhead roan was a good horse on a long trail, a better horse than the Ballards would have. The roan liked to travel and he had a taste for rough country, a hangover from his wild mustang days.

The Ballards had not expected to be followed and their trail was plain enough. Once in a while they made a pass at hiding their trail, but nothing that would even slow Bowdrie's pace.

It was not new country to him although he had ridden it but once before. South and west were some hills known locally as the Highbinders, a rough, broken country loved by Comanches because there was not a trail approaching them that could not be watched and there was ample water if one knew where to look.

Bowdrie thought as he rode. Clyde Ballard would be irritated. Clyde did not hold with killing unless it was in a stand-up fight or in the process of a holdup. An outlaw had to have places to hide and if people were set against you you'd never last long. Often enough they were indifferent, but never if you killed a neighbor or someone they respected.

Aaron Fobes was another type entirely. There was a streak of viciousness in him. Yet Fobes would not want to cross Clyde Ballard. Not even Luther Doyle would consider that, for Clyde was a good man with a gun.

No one of them considered the possibility of pursuit. They had been a long way from Benton when the shooting took place and there was no marshal in Miller's Crossing.

With the shrewdness of a man who had known many

trails, Chick Bowdrie could guess their thinking now. Clyde would be inwardly furious because the useless killing would make enemies and Miller's Crossing was a town they must avoid in future rides, and that meant some long, roundabout riding to get in and out of their hideout.

Bowdrie was in no hurry. He knew what awaited him at the ride's end and he was not riding for a record. It was almost ten days after the shooting before he rode up to the Sloacum place.

He drew rein outside the house as Tate Sloacum came striding up from the barn. "How's about some chuck?" Bowdrie suggested. "I've been thirty miles on an empty stomach."

" 'Light an' set," Sloacum said. "Turn your hoss into the corral. There's a bucket there alongside the well if you'd like to wash off some dust."

When he had washed, he ran his fingers through his hair and went up to the house. He had no Indian blood but he looked like an Apache and sometimes there was hesitance from those who did not know him. There was food in plenty but nobody talked during the meal. Eating was a serious business.

Tate Sloacum was the old man of the house, a West Virginia mountaineer by birth. He had two sons and a hawk-faced rider named Crilley. His wife was a slatternly woman with stringy red hair and a querulous voice. A daughter named Sary served them at table. She had red hair and a swish to her hips. With brothers like hers she was a girl who could get men killed.

Bowdrie was uncomfortable around women. He had known few of them well. He took in Sary with a glance and then averted his eyes and kept them averted. He knew trouble when he saw it.

At twenty-one Chick Bowdrie had been doing a man's work since he was twelve, herding cattle, breaking the wild stock, and riding the rough string. There had been little softness in his life and few friends. Once, when he could have been no older than eight, a man had stopped by the house for a meal. It was wild country with Indians about, and few traveled alone. This man did.

When Chick walked out to the corral with him he watched the man saddle up and step into the stirrup. For some reason, he hated to see him go. There had been something about the man that spoke of quiet strength.

Looking down from the saddle, the man had said, "Ride with honor, boy, ride with honor."

He did not know exactly what honor was but he never forgot the man and he was sure what the man had said was important.

A member of the Ballard gang had killed a man who befriended him, and he needed no more reason for hunting him down, and wanted no more. He had enlisted as a Ranger because it was practical. The law was coming to Texas and he preferred to ride with the law. McNelly, a shrewd judge of character, had recognized him for what he was. This young man was destined to be a hunter or one of the hunted, and McNelly reflected dryly that he'd rather hire him than lose men trying to catch him.

"We demand loyalty," he suggested. "Absolute loyalty."

"I ride for the brand," Bowdrie replied. "I never take a man's money without giving him what he's paid for."

"Where is your home?"

"Wherever I hang my hat," Bowdrie said. "I got nothing, nobody." Then he added, "I can read an' write."

"Your home?"

"Got no home. I was born near D'Hanis. Folks all gone. Mostly Injuns killed 'em."

"D'Hanis? Are you French?"

"Some. Some other blood, too. I don't know much about it. I growed up where most of the youngsters spoke French an' German as well as English."

"I know the area. Do you speak Spanish?"

"I get by. I worked cows with Mexican riders. We got along."

That was how it began. Bowdrie thought back to it now, thinking he had taken the right turn, on the right side of the law, and he knew how easy it would have been to go the other way. Sooner or later he might have killed the wrong man.

"Need a place to hole up," he told Sloacum, "a quiet place where a man can rest and let his horse eat grass."

Sloacum gestured toward the hills. "We call 'em the Highbinders. Used to be Comanches. Mostly they're gone now." He gestured toward the house. "Come up when you've unsaddled, and we'll have some grub on."

That was before he sat down. He ate well, simple food, well-cooked. The two boys disappeared when supper was over but Crilley lingered, stropping his knife on his boot sole.

"I seen you somewheres afore," he said to Bowdrie.

"I been someplace before, but I never seen you."

He did not remember ever seeing Crilley and did not care if Crilley had seen him. The cowboy might have seen him when he rode for Whipple and could take the information to Ballard if he wished. Bowdrie had to find a trail and Crilley might make it for him. Nor did he care if the Ballards were ready for him. He was ready for them, too.

He got up and Sloacum glanced at him. "You can sleep in the haymow. Ain't got an extry bed."

"I've slept in 'em before. Better'n most."

He left the house and went to the barn, where he found a big hayloft half-filled with fresh-smelling hay. He spread his blankets and bedded down, the big wide hayloft door open to the out-of-doors and showing a wide stretch of starlit sky.

He could have been asleep for scarcely more than an hour when he was suddenly awake, gun in hand. He could not have explained how the gun got there. It was one of those instinctive actions that come to men who live close to danger. Weapons become so much a part of their existence that they no longer seem remarkable.

Then he recalled what had awakened him. The sound of a horseshoe clicking against stone. Sitting up, he strained his ears to hear, and it came again, the muffled hoof-falls of a horse and a creak of saddle leather.

Keeping to the darkness away from the open door, he moved softly to where he could see out.

Chick Bowdrie had found little time for romance in his life or he, instead of Tom Ballard, might have been meeting Sary near the corral, but he witnessed their greeting, a healthy if not soulful kiss. If there was no delicacy in the kiss there was no lack of earthy appreciation in it.

Chick had not come to witness kisses, so he stood waiting. He had recognized Ballard from other days.

"Anybody been around?" Tom asked.

"Uh-huh. Stranger passin' through. Sleepin' in the loft right now. He was astin' Pa for a place where there was water where he could lay up for a while. Pappy thinks he's on the dodge."

"What's he look like?"

"He ain't no Ranger, if that's what you're scared of. Although he does have one of those new Winchesters like they carry. Looks more like a gunhand. Dark, narrow features. Nose like a hawk. Eyes blacker than a well bottom. Packs two tied-down six-shooters. Walks straight an' fast. He's ridin' a mean-lookin' strawberry roan."

Tom Ballard drew a breath. "Got a little scar, has he? Like a thin sort of dimple below his cheekbone?"

"That's him! Who is he?"

"Bowdrie, Chick Bowdrie. He's the man who killed Pete Drago a while back."

"Is he huntin' you?"

"I hope not. Why should he be? He's kind of on the outlaw side himself, from what I hear. Just ridin' through, most likely."

The rest was unimportant. Bowdrie tiptoed back to

his bed and stretched out. He was fast asleep within minutes.

He was dipping his head in the water bucket when Sary appeared the following morning. He shook the water from his hair, then wiped his face and hands on the roller towel beside the back door.

"I'm huntin' a place to lie up for a while," he suggested. "I'd be obliged for any ideas."

"Nothin' around here." She eyed him with speculative eyes. "Would you come a-callin' if you was close by?"

Bowdrie admitted he was no hand with women but he knew a trail when he saw it. His bloodhound's instinct told him what to say. "Why else would an hombre want to stay in this country?"

Sary finished drawing her bucket from the well. "There's the Highbinders, them low, brush-covered hills you see out past the barn. There's water there, and a few deer. A body could kill him an antelope if he needed meat. Or even a steer, so long as it isn't one of ours. Nobody out here kills his own beef," she added.

At the table they ate thick steaks cooked well-done and drank black bean coffee. There were cookies, too. Ma Sloacum could cook and bake.

Crilley, Bowdrie noted before Tate Sloacum even spoke, was nowhere around. "Where's Joe? Ain't like him to miss breakfast."

"He got his coffee, then taken off to the hills before sunup," Ma explained.

Almost an hour later Crilley rode into the canyon where the Ballards were holed up. He dropped from his horse at the cabin and glanced over at Aaron Fobes, who stood beside the cabin door.

"I got bad news," he said.

Clyde Ballard came to the door, Luther Doyle and Northup behind him.

"What news?" Fobes demanded.

"Chick Bowdrie's eatin' breakfast over at Sloacum's."

"What's that to us?" Clyde asked.

"Fobes here, he killed Noah Whipple over at Miller's, didn't he? Well, when Bowdrie rode in the other night I couldn't place him, then it come to me. He pulled into Whipple's a while back with some bullets in him. They nursed him back to health, an' he stayed on, ridin' for Whipple for a few months. I hear he sets store by that family."

Aaron Fobes looked sullen. "Bowdrie ain't got no call to come huntin' me. Anyway, I can take him or any two like him."

"You'd better hightail it, Aaron," Clyde suggested. "The way I hear it, he's somethin' to see with those guns of his."

"How'll he find me?" Fobes looked over at Crilley. "Unless you tell him."

"I ain't tellin' nothin' to nobody."

He knew Fobes and the thought did not make him happy. Suddenly he wished he hadn't been in so much of a hurry to ride over and tell him. He should have let well enough alone. Yet he liked Clyde Ballard and Clyde was a feudist—a fight with one of his men was a fight for all. Crilley had never liked Fobes. He was a mean, difficult man.

"He'll find you," Clyde said. "I've heard of him and he could trail a rattler across a flat rock, but if anybody is huntin' him they have to burn the stump and sift the ashes before they find him."

When Crilley did not appear for breakfast, Bowdrie decided there was but one reason for his absence. Obviously it was something of which the family knew nothing, and such absences were not the usual thing for Crilley, or no comment would have been made.

Why, then, had he gone? Only one thing out of the ordinary had happened at Sloacum's—his own arrival. The night before, Crilley had been sure he had seen Bowdrie somewhere before. Obviously he had remembered where and had ridden to inform the Ballards.

If he had ridden into the Highbinders, he would leave a trail, and where a horse had gone, Bowdrie could follow. A half-hour after breakfast he was in the saddle, riding east. When well out from the ranch, he swung in a wide circle until he picked up the sign of Crilley's horse.

He rode swiftly, making good time. Ahead of him the trail dipped into a dry wash and turned away from the hills. He followed until the trail came to a clear stream of water, less than a foot deep and flowing over a sand-and-gravel bottom.

Bowdrie swung down for a drink and let his horse drink, on the theory that a man never knew what might happen. He rode upstream first and was lucky. He found several hoofprints the water had not yet washed away. Riding or walking in the water is not always a means of losing one's trail. Bowdrie knew a dozen ways of following such a trail. Horseshoes could scar rocks even underwater.

Several times he reined in to study the country and the Highbinders, which were close now.

His thoughts returned to Joanie, clinging to his arm when he rode to town looking for Noah. She had not known about her father then, although her mother was worried that her husband had not returned as planned.

"Bring me something from town, Chick! Please!"

What did you bring a girl from town? That was more of a problem than Crilley's trail. He must find her something, some little knickknack. He would . . .

He saw a hoofprint in the clay bank where Crilley's horse had left the water. The trail turned back along the bank, weaving in and out of thick brush.

He never heard the shot.

A wicked blow on the head knocked him from the saddle, unconscious before he hit the ground. Something tore at him with angry fingers—and he hit, sagged, and hung.

When his eyes opened he was staring into a black,

glassy world. Something that moved, flowed, a glassy world that mirrored a face, his face.

He started to move, but brush crackled and he felt again that sagging feeling. Slowly he became aware. He had fallen from his horse and was suspended in the brush above the stream's edge. His foot felt cold, and looking down, he saw one boot toe trailed in the water. He lifted it clear.

Carefully he looked around. He had fallen into brush which partly supported his weight, but his gunbelt had caught on an old snag, which had helped keep him clear of the water, where he might have drowned, shallow though it was.

Nearby was a branch that looked sturdier than the others. He grasped it, tested it, and slowly, carefully lifted himself clear. Climbing out of his precarious position was a shaky business, but he managed.

He crawled higher on the bank. He had been dry-gulched. They had waylaid him and shot him from the saddle, leaving him for dead.

He still had his guns. One remained in its holster; the other had fallen on the bank. He picked it up and wiped the clay from it, testing the action.

It was almost sundown, which meant he had been unconscious for hours. Delicately his fingers felt the furrow in his scalp. The blood had dried and caked his hair. Better not disturb it. He knelt by the stream and washed the blood from his face, however.

Looking about, he found his hat and placed it gingerly on his head.

There was no sign of his horse but there was still enough light for tracking. When he had fallen, the roan had bolted. Weaving his way through the brush and then a grove of small trees, he suddenly glimpsed the horse standing in a small meadow, looking at him.

When the hammerhead saw him it nickered softly, and actually seemed glad to see him. His Winchester was still in the saddle scabbard. The horse even took a couple of steps toward him. When he had first caught the roan from the wild bunch, his friends advised him to turn it loose. "That's no kind of a horse, Chick. Look at that head. And he's got a mean look to him. Turn him loose or shoot him. That horse is a killer!"

They had been right, of course. The roan was such a savage bucker that when he threw a rider he turned and went for him with intent to kill. He was lean, rawboned, and irritable, yet Bowdrie had developed an affection for him. Pet the roan and he would try to bite you. Curry him and he'd kick. But on a trail he would go all day and all night with a sort of ugly determination. Bowdrie had never known a horse with so much personality, and all of it bad. Nor did the roan associate much with other horses. He seemed to like being in a corral where they were, but he held himself aloof.

Of one thing Bowdrie was sure. No stranger was going to mount the roan. As for horse thieves, only one had tried to steal the roan, for in a herd of horses the roan would be the last anyone would select. The one attempt had been by a man in a hurry and the roan was there.

The horse thief jerked free of the tie-rope and leaped into the saddle. The roan spun like a top and then bucked and the would-be rider was piled into the water trough and his screams brought Bowdrie and the marshal running, for the roan had grabbed the thief's shoulder in his teeth.

Bowdrie took the bridle, spoke to the horse, then mounted and rode away. The thief, badly shaken and bloody, was helped from the trough. Aside from the savage bite, he had a broken shoulder.

"What was *that*?" the outlaw whined. "What . . .?"

"That was Chick Bowdrie an' that outlaw roan he rides." The marshal kept one hand on his prisoner while looking down the street after Bowdrie. "They deserve each other," he added. "They're two of a kind."

Bowdrie found the camp by its firelight. It was artfully hidden but the light reflected from rocks and there was a small glow in the night.

On foot Chick Bowdrie walked down the grassy bank toward the fire. Aaron Fobes was talking. "No call for Clyde to get huffy," he complained. "I just got him before he could get me."

Meat was roasting over the fire, and the two men were doing a foolish thing. They were looking into the flames as they talked, which ruins the vision for immediate night work. There was no sign of the Ballards, nor of Northup.

"Maybe he didn't have a chance, but what difference does that make?"

"Get up, Fobes!"

Fobes started as if touched by a spark from the fire; then slowly he began to rise.

"You in this, Doyle?" Bowdrie's black eyes kept both men in view. "If you ain't, back up an' stay out!"

"I ride with him," Luther Doyle said.

Fobes had reached for his gun as he came erect, and Doyle, who had not quite made up his mind, was slower. Yet Doyle was the deadlier of the two and Bowdrie's first shot knocked him staggering and he fell backward over the saddles. The second and third shots took Aaron Fobes in the throat and face. Fobes fell forward into the fire, scattering it. Doyle got off a quick shot that knocked the left-hand gun from Bowdrie's grip, leaving his hand numb. Doyle fired again and missed, taking a slug in the chest. He fell forward and lay still.

Chick walked over and retrieved his gun, holstering it, rubbing his left hand against his pants to restore the feeling. Then he caught Fobes by the back of his shirt and lifted him free of the fire. The man was dead.

Bowdrie got his canteen from his horse and lifted Doyle's head to give him a swallow.

The wounded man's eyes flickered. "He wasn't worth it, but I rode with him. No hard feelings?"

"None," Bowdrie replied. "Next time you better choose better comp'ny. You could get yourself killed."

He opened the wounded man's shirt. The one low

down on the left side looked ugly, but the other shot had hit Doyle's heavy metal belt buckle and glanced off, ripping the skin across his stomach for a good six inches, but the wound was only a bad scratch.

"Am I bad off?"

"Not too bad. You'll live, most likely. I'll patch you up some when I get time. Now we got comp'ny."

He thumbed cartridges into his guns, holstering the left one. His hand was still numb, but if necessary . . .

"What d'you plan to do?" Doyle asked.

"Take the Ballards," Bowdrie said. "I'm a Texas Ranger."

"Bowdrie? A *Ranger?*"

"Since Fobes killed Noah Whipple." He grabbed Doyle's handkerchief and shoved it into his mouth, but the outlaw spat it out. "I won't holler," Doyle said. "If I do, there'll be shootin'."

They waited in silence, listening to the approaching horses.

"Watch Northup," Doyle said. "I don't want Clyde shot up."

Three men rode into the firelight and started to swing down. One was on the ground before they saw anything amiss.

"Hold it, Ballard!" Bowdrie said. "This is Chick Bowdrie and I'm a Texas Ranger. I'm arrestin' you for the Benton bank job!"

Clyde Ballard stood very still. His brother was beside him, only a few feet away, and Northup was a good ten feet to their left. They were full in the firelight and Bowdrie was in half-darkness beyond the fire. Clyde could see Fobes's body, realizing for the first time that the man was dead, not sleeping. He could only see the legs of Luther Doyle but it was obvious the man was out of action.

Nobody had ever accused Clyde Ballard of lack of courage. He was hard, tough, and at times reckless, but even a child could see that somebody could die here, and Tom was only a kid.

"He means it, Clyde," Doyle said. "He's hell on wheels with them guns and we might get him but he'd get all of us. We can beat this one in court."

It was wise counsel, Clyde knew. It would not be easy to convict them of the Benton job, as they had all been masked. Moreover, it was miles to prison and they had friends.

"What about the Miller Crossing killing?" Clyde asked.

"Fobes did that. He's dead. As far as I'm concerned, that's a closed chapter. You can have it any way you want it. Doyle can live if we get him to a doctor."

Ballard hesitated. With a single move he could turn the evening into a red-laced bit of hell, but what the Ranger said was true and he had been careful never to buck the Rangers.

"You've got us cold-decked, Bowdrie. I'm dropping my guns." His hands went carefully to his belt buckle. "Tom?"

The guns dropped, and Tom's followed.

"Like hell!" Cousin Northup's tone was wild. "No damn Ranger is takin' me in!"

Bowdrie's gun was in his hand but he hesitated a split second as Northup's pistol cleared leather; then he shot him. The Ballards stood, hands lifted. Bowdrie looked at them for a moment, then holstered his gun.

"Cousin was always a mite hasty," Clyde said, and then added, "We might have gotten into that, but one of us would surely have gotten hisself killed, and there was Luther here. If we killed you, he'd have no show a-tall. An' we'd have nobody who knew we'd surrendered ourselves."

Bowdrie gathered their guns and hung the belts on his saddle.

"If we can get him to Sloacum's," Clyde said, "that ol' man's most as good as a doctor. He might fix him up until we can get help."

They got Luther into the saddle and started for the ranch. Bowdrie had three prisoners and a report to write up. He'd never written a report and did not know what to say.

And he would have to stop in town to buy something for Joanie.

"You fellers could help me," he said to Clyde. "If you was asked to buy something in town for a girl, maybe sixteen, what would you get for her?"

"Well," Clyde said, "I'd . . ."

It was a long way to town.

HISTORICAL NOTE:

JOHN COFFEE HAYS, TEXAS RANGER

Born at Little Cedar Lick, Tennessee, in 1817, Jack Hays, as he was called, went to live with an uncle after the death of his father. He became a surveyor when only fifteen, and in 1836 left Mississippi to fight for the independence of Texas. One of his first tasks was to help bury the bodies of the 350 men of Fannin's command who were lined up and shot down after their surrender. The death of those men left an indelible impression on Hays.

Hays became captain of one of the first companies of Texas Rangers, organized to defend Texas against rampaging parties of Comanches as well as outlaws and guerrilla fighters from over the border.

The Comanches were making raids deep into the settled portions of Texas, and Hays was one of those who led Rangers against them. At the Battle of Plum Creek his Rangers met a much larger force of Comanches. The Indians, accustomed to single-shot weapons, had contrived to defeat several parties sent against them by first feinting an attack and then, when the defenders had fired their weapons, attacking, sure that the guns of the white men were empty. Riding with speed, and no finer horsemen ever existed, they could discharge twenty to thirty arrows while a man was reloading his rifle. On this occasion, however, Hays had armed his men with the newly invented Colt pistol.

The Comanches feinted a charge, the Rangers fired, and then the Comanches struck in force. And the Rangers with their repeating weapons continued to fire. Outnumbered four to one, Hays's Rangers defeated the Comanches, leaving almost half of them dead upon the field.

Later, after taking part in the war with Mexico, Hays led an expedition west along the border to San Diego, California. He made several attempts to make a treaty with the Apaches without any great success. He had made contact with a white renegade living among the Apaches, but an unexpected attack by Mexican soldiers made the Indians suspicious.

In San Francisco, Walker was elected sheriff, still later he led an armed force against the Paiutes and defeated them in a battle near Pyramid Lake.

Colonel Jack Hays died peacefully on San Jacinto Day in 1883 in Oakland, California, a city he had had a hand in founding.

Although Cullen Baker is usually credited with the invention of the fast draw as a tactic, Jack Hays killed a barroom toublemaker with a fast draw in 1836. I do not know that he ever used it again.

Where Buzzards Fly

The Mexican's rifle lay over his horse's body, his pistol near his hand. He had gone out fighting, riddled with bullets. His flat, knife-scarred face was unforgettable, his eyes wide and unafraid, staring up to a brassy sky.

"Well, Zaparo," Bowdrie said aloud, "it looks like they've washed out your trail."

His eyes swept the narrow gray gravel-and-sand trail that lay along the bottom of the arroyo, littered now with the bodies of men and horses, all dead.

Fourteen men had gone out fighting, fourteen men killed in what must have been minutes. These had been hard, desperate men and they would not have gone easily. This had been an ambush, of course, carefully planned, perfectly timed.

He who conceived the idea had a mind to reckon with. He was cold, cruel, utterly ruthless. Walking slowly along the line of fallen men, Bowdrie stared bleakly at the litter of bodies scattered along three hundred yards of trail. Above, in slow, patient circles, the buzzards were waiting. They had seen such things before and knew their time would come.

Yesterday, probably in the late afternoon, there had been a moment here of blood-steeped inferno, flashes of gunfire, and the thunder of heavy rifles.

Zaparo had moved fast after his swift raid on the

ranches and missions, moving along a preplanned route, but somebody had sold him out. Other men, more bloodthirsty than he, had waited with a welcome of gunfire. It was not a nice thing to see or to contemplate. In the hard world to which Bowdrie had been born and in which he lived, death was an old story, and the possibility of death by violence rode along with every traveler. The death of men in gun battles he could accept, but ambush and murder were another thing. In any event, it was his job.

When he had become a Ranger he had known what lay before him, but this was the worst he had seen. Unless he was failing to read the signs, the betrayer had himself been betrayed. That last man, who hung back behind the others, had left his gun in his holster, and he had been shot in the back at close quarters. Whoever planned this crime had not planned to trust the man who betrayed others. He lay dead along with the rest.

For three hours Bowdrie studied the scene, and he was stumped. There were those who said Bowdrie could trail a snake across a flat rock, but now he could find no evidence.

No cartridge shells remained that could have been left by the attackers, no cigarette butts. All had been gathered up with painstaking care. Every track had been brushed out with mesquite branches. Not one iota of evidence remained, nothing that might lead him to the perpetrators. Yet there is no such thing as a perfect crime. There are only imperfect investigators.

Seated on a flat rock, Chick brooded over the situation.

Obviously the killers had known well in advance, for the site had been well-chosen. There had been, Bowdrie calculated, at least seven men in the ambush party, and those seven must have been among the deadliest marksmen along the border. They had been facing fourteen Mexicans who could and would fight. Hence the seven, if there were that many, had to have been carefully picked. That, he decided, was his first clue.

If he could not trail the killers on the ground, he would trail them with his mind.

Seven dangerous, hard-as-nails men, all ready to kill. To lead them, a man would have to be harder, colder, even more dangerous. He would have to be able to handle the other six, and he would have to enjoy their confidence. Such men were rare.

Scanning in his mind the Rangers' fugitive list, he could find no man that fit. John Wesley Hardin might have been a possibility, but Hardin's killings had never been for profit but were a result of feuds or similar situations. Nor was he a planner such as this man had been.

First he must discover who had been involved. What men had been seen in the country around who might have been involved? He must locate one or two possibilities and track them back through the past few weeks to see if they had come together at any time.

Of course, there was another way.

The betrayer was dead, but his betraying need not be at an end. Mounting his roan, he walked back along the line of battle until he came to the body of the betrayer. Zaparo was no longer important. This man was.

Swinging down, Chick Bowdrie went through the dead man's pockets. Nothing had been taken from him. The man's name was Juan Pirón. It was hand-tooled on his belt. He was short and thick with a ragged scar over an eyebrow, and he had ridden a mouse-colored mustang with one white stocking. Pirón looked like a hard man to get along with.

If Juan Pirón had betrayed Zaparo, he had betrayed him to someone he knew, someone he believed could cope with the bandit chief. At some time in the past few weeks or months they had met, but at sometime in the past few days Pirón must have met the killer boss or one of his men to supply the information as to their route.

There lay a chance. To trail Juan Pirón, check with

everyone he had known, to find out where he hung out, what he had been doing.

Mounting his hammerhead roan, Bowdrie let the long-legged horse turn back up the arroyo trail. The roan took his own pace, a shambling, loose-limbed trot, and the miles began to fall behind.

Zaparo's gang had looted two missions and some Mexican ranches of nearly one hundred and fifty thousand dollars in gold and money, most of this altar fixtures from the missions. They had fled across the border to the north, and the Rurales had alerted the Rangers.

The Rangers, as usual, had business of their own, and McNelly detached Bowdrie to see what he could find. What he found was totally unexpected.

It was nearly dusk when Bowdrie rode into the wide ranch-yard of Tom Katch's K-Bar. A couple of hands loafed in front of the bunkhouse, and Tom Katch himself, an easygoing man with friendly eyes, was sitting on the veranda. Rangers were always welcome at the K-Bar, and there was always coffee, a meal, and a bed.

"Howdy, Chick!" Katch leaned his massive forearms on the rail as Bowdrie stepped down from the saddle. "What brings you thisaway?"

"Zaparo."

"He on the rampage again? Somebody ought to round him up with a rope."

"Somebody has. With a bullet."

"Dead, is he? What happened?"

Bowdrie dropped into a chair beside Katch and accepted a cup of coffee from a Mexican girl. He dropped his hat on the floor and sipped coffee. Then he put his cup down and explained as briefly as possible, telling only about the ambush, fourteen dead bodies, and the dead horses.

"Clean job," Bowdrie added. "Not the least hint of a trail."

"Hey, boys!" Katch called out. "Zaparo's been killed!"

The hands trooped up to the porch. The first one seated himself on the steps, looking toward them. He was a hard-featured, wiry, and whipcord young man. "We ain't met," he said to Bowdrie. "My name's Ferd Cassidy."

Katch waved a hand at the others. "Hawkins, Broughten, Werner, and Cadieux. Top hands ever' man of them, Bowdrie, and on this outfit they'd better be."

Cassidy agreed. "He works the hell out of us. You're lucky to have a job that beats punchin' cows."

"Well, nobody much cares about a lot of Mexican outlaws," Hawkins commented. "Who d'you reckon did the killin'?"

Bowdrie shrugged. "No idea who did it. Must be a new outfit. But you're wrong about nobody caring. We care. And an outfit that kills like that might kill anybody. We don't hold with lawbreakers, no matter who they are or who they kill."

"Some other Mexican outfit could have trailed 'em," Broughten suggested, "or Apaches."

Bowdrie nodded. "Could be." He paused a moment. "Any of you hombres seen a short, stocky Mexican with a scar over one eye?"

Did Hawkins stiffen a little? Or was it imagination? "Can't say I have," he said, "but I never knowed many Mexicans, anyway."

"Got a pickup order on him," Bowdrie lied. "Some shootin' over Concho way. He prob'ly headed east, anyway."

"Lots of Mexican cowboys workin' this range," Katch suggested. "Right good hands, some of them."

At daybreak Bowdrie rolled out of his bunk and poured water from a wooden bucket into a basin and bathed his face and hands. He threw out the water and refilled the bucket at the well.

He wiped the dust from his boots and the silver spurs given him long ago by a Mexican he had befriended. He dug a fresh shirt from his pack and donned it, a black-and-white-checked shirt. He wore a black neckerchief and black pants. He checked his Colts, returned each to its holster, and taking up his Winchester, he went outside.

"Better have some breakfast," Cassidy suggested as he walked past, headed for the corral.

Tom Katch was alone at the table when Bowdrie went inside. Katch was a big man, six-feet-four and weighing a good two hundred and thirty.

"If there's anything we can do, let us know. Cassidy is a good man on a trail and he likes a fight, but all of us are ready to take a hand if we're needed."

Katch talked while Bowdrie ate, sitting with a cup of coffee over the remains of his breakfast. "That Mexican you spoke of? Did he have a name?"

"We didn't have a name," Bowdrie said, "just a description. He was a horse thief who got caught and killed a man." He was making up the story as he went along, not wanting to tip his hand too much. "I can't bother with him now. This ambush is the important thing."

Once he was back on the trail, Bowdrie slowed the roan to a walk. He had little to work with aside from the knowledge that it would require a hard lot of men and the fact that he knew who had betrayed the Zaparo outfit. The loot had been taken away on the pack mules that carried it, and those mules must be somewhere around. He knew they were mules from the hoofprints at the scene, and he had back-trailed the bandits for a mile or so.

The loot must be hidden for the time, and such a lot of men and mules could not travel far without being seen.

Mentally he shaped a map of the area, bounded on the south by the Rio Grande, and with the arroyo where the ambush occurred as the center. North and west of that arroyo was the range where the K-Bar ran their cattle, and south to the river it was rough, half-desert country where few men ventured. East there was twenty miles of rough country and then the small village of Pasamonte. There was something else. Not over eight miles from the arroyo was the cantina and roadhouse of Pedro Padilla.

The cantina was the favored stopping place for cowhands, wet Mexicans from the Rio Grande crossing, and all manner of wayfarers. Aside from Pasamonte it was the only place a man could buy a drink or a meal.

The cantina was built on the ruins of an old mission, a long, low, rambling building surrounding a stone-paved patio. It utilized two walls and the floor of the ancient building, three sides of which were the cantina, and the fourth was reserved for the Padilla family.

If any news was floating around, Pedro Padilla would have heard it. If any strangers had come into the country, he would know. If mules had passed, he would have seen them. The question was, would he tell a Ranger? Or anybody?

What must Bowdrie find out? Who was the leader of the attackers? Where had they gone from the arroyo? Where had Juan Pirón met with the leader of the ambushers? How had he transmitted the final information as to route, and so on? By what route had the killers arrived at the arroyo?

All could turn on Pirón himself. He was the one link between the bandits and their murderers.

The cantina basked in the hot desert sun. Leaving his horse in the shade of some cottonwoods, Bowdrie entered the spacious, low-raftered room that was the cantina itself. Strings of peppers hung everywhere, and there were two ollas of fresh cold water, each with a gourd dipper. A dozen tables and a bar, a floor of freshly swept flagstones.

Padilla was a paunchy Mexican with a large black mustache and a wary eye, the latter no doubt because he had several attractive daughters. He wore a huge old-fashioned pistol, perhaps for the same reason.

He not only had daughters, Bowdrie perceived, but granddaughters as well, and a wife that would make two of him. Dropping into a chair, Bowdrie ordered a cold beer, suggesting to Padilla that he join him and have one himself.

A desultory conversation began, inhibited somewhat by the Ranger's badge on his vest, a conversation that covered the heat, the lack of rain, the condition of the range and its cattle, as well as the difficulties of conducting a business so far from the law.

"No doubt," Bowdrie suggested, "many bad men come as well as the good. You are close to the border."

"*Sí!* They come, they spend money, they go! I know none of them, and do not wish to know!"

One of Padilla's daughters was wiping a table nearby, and Chick watched her.

"Juan Pirón comes here often?" he asked casually, aware that she was listening.

"Pirón?" Padilla shrugged. "I do not know him. He is a vaquero?"

"That, too, maybe. . . . He is a *bandido*, I think."

Padilla's daughter had paused an instant at the name. She knew the name, he was sure. More likely that Padilla knew Zaparo.

"It is bad about Zaparo," he said thoughtfully. He took a swallow of the beer.

Padilla glanced at him, then away. "Zaparo? I have heard of him."

"*Sí.* It is a bad thing. To be killed is bad, to be ambushed—"

The broom handle hit the floor. Bowdrie's eyes went to the girl. She was staring wide-eyed at him. "Zaparo? He was killed? His men too?"

"All," he replied, "all are gone. They never had a chance."

Padilla was staring, disbelief in his eyes. His daughter dropped to her knees, clasping her apron in her fingers. "Not the young one! Not he of the curly hair! Do not tell me the young one with the smile, the—!"

Bowdrie's memory was good, and no such Mexican had been among the dead. Yet, how could that be? An ambush with one man escaping? The sort of men he had been picturing would never let anyone escape. There was something wrong here, something . . .

"Fourteen men were dead on the ground, Chiquita," he explained.

"The Rurales?" Padilla asked.

"No, it was other *bandidos*, gringo *bandidos* perhaps. I do not know." His eyes studied the innkeeper. "Zaparo is dead, *señor*, and you were his friend, I think. Now it does not matter except that I must find those who killed him. A killing is an evil thing no matter who is killed, and his killers were evil men."

He paused. "I think this Juan Pirón betrayed Zaparo." He caught Padilla's wrist. "Do you know who that someone was, *amigo*? Have you seen Pirón talking to someone? Even here, perhaps?"

There was a brief flare of realization in Padilla's eyes, but he merely shrugged. "Perhaps he talks here. I do not remember."

Bowdrie glanced at the girl, still on her knees where she had fallen. "Chiquita, if your lover was a man of Zaparo, and if he looked as you have said, he was not among the dead. I remember each face, each man. He was not among them."

"*Gracias, señor!*" She got to her feet, eyes bright with happiness.

Padilla got up suddenly and left the room. Chick caught the girl's hand. "Chiquita, you can help me. Zaparo was not a good man, yet not so bad as some. He stole precious things from churches in Sonora. They must be found and returned. Your lover was not killed, so he will come to you, no? If he does, send him to me. He can help me."

"You would not betray him, *señor*? To the Rurales? We are to be married soon."

"I wish to speak to him, that is all. What he has done was in Mexico, but now he can change. Zaparo is dead, but those who killed him must be found. Your man can help me."

*   *   *

Bowdrie awakened suddenly, hours later, lying across his bed above the cantina. Music sounded from below, but it was not that which awakened him. A dozen horses were tied at the hitching rail outside the gate of the patio. From where he lay he could see across the patio and into the lighted window opposite.

Ferd Cassidy suddenly appeared in the room, but moving as if he had just risen from a seat. Then Broughten came into the room with Hawkins. Only nine or ten miles from the K-Bar this was undoubtedly a hangout for the men from the ranch.

Bowdrie went to the basin, still in the half-light from the window opposite, and splashed cold water on his face. Then he combed his hair before picking up his hat. As he started for the door, a surreptitious movement arrested his attention and he froze in position, watching.

The Mexican girl, Chiquita, was leading a saddled horse toward the gate, obviously not wishing to be discovered. He waited an instant, then stepped out into the night. The girl was outside the gate, where she slipped into the saddle and started walking her horse along the trail.

At almost the instant she got into the saddle, the dark figure of a man showed against the lighted window opposite, then vanished. As Bowdrie started for the gate himself, he saw the man mount and ride after the girl. Where could she be going at such an hour? Who was following her?

Stepping quickly into the stable, Bowdrie saddled and bridled the roan. Gathering the reins, he stepped into the saddle and followed them down the trail, keeping to the grassy shoulder. Within a few minutes he glimpsed the man ahead; then he seemed to vanish.

Worried, Bowdrie reached the spot only to discover that the desert broke away into the steep bank of a wash. Starting down the side, he glimpsed the outline of a rider against the night, a rider some distance off, but who could only be Chiquita. What had become of the man following her?

Glancing right and left into the deeper shadows, he decided that rider must have ridden either up or down the wash, knowing perhaps that this wash intercepted the trail farther along. Bowdrie chose to follow Chiquita up the steep opposite bank. She rode straight on as though to a goal, and Chick had an idea of whom she planned to meet.

They rode for nearly an hour; then a faint glimmer of firelight showed. By now they were in a remote region of canyons and weird rock formations where such a fire could not be seen for any distance. Bowdrie, following warily, glimpsed it only occasionally when he topped out on high ground or when the rocks stood apart to offer greater visibility. Chiquita rode directly to the fire and slid from her horse.

Bowdrie studied the terrain. What had become of the rider who followed her? Had that rider realized Bowdrie was behind them?

Tying the roan to a mesquite bush, he crept through the cacti and mesquite until he could, from behind a rock, overlook the situation.

The young Mexican who held the girl in his arms could only be a henchman of Zaparo's. They were talking in Spanish but the air was clear and Bowdrie was close enough to hear every word.

"It is what you feared," she was saying. "Something has happened! Zaparo is dead! All of them are dead! They were attacked by other outlaws and killed! All of them!"

"*Zaparo?* But *how?* Who could have known their way?"

"The gringo with the black hat, the one who looks like an Apache, he says it was Juan Pirón who betrayed them."

"Ah? I am not surprised. But he was killed also?"

"The gringo says they are all dead, that they had no

further use for Pirón, and did not trust him. And now they have the loot!"

"I care nothing for that!" he said indignantly. "But *Zaparo*! There was a man! He was my friend, also, and to be betrayed by such a man?"

"The gringo wishes to talk to you. He promises you no harm. He wishes only to find the gringo outlaws."

The Mexican shook his head. "I know nothing, Chiquita!"

Their voices became lower, and then after a quick kiss Chiquita gave him a package of food and got back into the saddle. Turning her horse, she rode into darkness.

Bowdrie was in a quandary. Here was his chance to talk to the young Mexican, and there might never be another. On the other hand, the unknown rider might follow Chiquita. Had he also overheard? Or had he come this far?

He made his decision quickly. He would do both.

He spoke, hoping his voice would carry no farther than the young Mexican. "Stand where you are! I am a friend!"

The Mexican rooted himself in his tracks, but turned slowly to face him.

"I am the gringo Chiquita mentioned, and I must talk with you, but we must ride also, for Chiquita is in danger."

"Chiquita? In danger? I will get my horse."

Warily Chick watched him go, then circled the fire beyond the reach of its light. He saw no good place where a watcher might have been, and if there had been one, he was gone.

"Leave the fire. There is nothing for it to burn and there is no time."

Bowdrie led the way; then the Mexican closed up beside him and Bowdrie explained about the follower he had glimpsed. Then he asked, "What do you know of Pirón?"

"He was cousin to Zaparo but I did not trust him. I

followed once when he met with two men, but could not see their faces. Zaparo would not believe he was a traitor. He became very angry with me."

"How did it happen you were not with them?"

"My father, *señor*, he is ill. When he became better I rode to see Chiquita, but also hoping she could tell what happened to Zaparo. He had been gone too long, and at the cantina they hear everything."

Suddenly they heard a scream, quickly choked off. The young Mexican slapped spurs to his horse and was gone like a shot. Bowdrie could only follow.

He saw them suddenly, two struggling figures in the road, but at the sound of the rushing horses the man threw the girl from him and grabbed for his pistol. Chick drew and fired, and the man dropped his gun and staggered, dropping to his knees.

Bowdrie hit the ground on the run and saw the young Mexican go to Chiquita. She fell into his arms, moaning with fright, and Chick struck a match with his thumbnail. The wounded man was Hawkins.

"What did you jump me for?" Hawkins did not seem badly hurt, but it was too dark to see. "Can't a feller have a little fun without you hornin' in?"

"Not when the girl doesn't want him," Bowdrie replied.

"Huh! You'd help one of Zaparo's outlaws rather'n an American?"

The moon, rising now above the mountain ridge, provided small light. How, Bowdrie wondered, had Hawkins known the Mexican was one of Zaparo's gang? Such gossip might be going around, of course. Still . . .

"Mount up," he said. "We'll ride back to the cantina. And you, Hawkins, consider yourself my prisoner."

"Me?" Hawkins was startled. "A prisoner? What for?"

"Mount up," Bowdrie replied. "I think you're just the man I've been lookin' for."

Hawkins became suddenly quiet. "So?" he said. Nor did he utter another word during the ride back to the cantina. Bowdrie took him through a back way, guided by Chiquita, to one of Padilla's spare rooms, where he handcuffed him to the bed.

Bowdrie's hasty shot had done little damage. It had, judging from a quick examination, hit Hawkins's large belt buckle at an angle, glanced off, and ripped his shirt at the elbow, scratching the skin and momentarily numbing his arm and hand.

"You were lucky," Bowdrie said briefly, "or maybe you weren't, depending on whether you prefer a bullet to a rope."

"What's that mean?" Hawkins demanded.

Leaving him handcuffed, Bowdrie went into the cantina, where Broughten was watching a poker game and a half-dozen others were hanging about. One of them was Ferd Cassidy.

Chick nodded to him. "When you get ready to ride," he commented, "don't wait for Hawkins. He's under arrest."

Broughten turned sharply and Cassidy put his glass down on the table.

"What's he done?" Cassidy asked.

"He followed one of Padilla's girls into the desert and got rough with her." Bowdrie paused, then added, "While I have him, I'd better speak to him on some other matters."

"What matters?" Cassidy's eyes were cold and ugly.

There was a tenseness in the man that went beyond what could be expected. Suddenly Bowdrie was wondering. Why not the K-Bar outfit? A tough lot, close to the scene, yet so far as he knew, nothing of the kind had ever been held against them before. Of course, there was always the first time, and if they were tipped off to the amount of loot . . .

A man came in the door, glanced around, taking in the tableau with casual interest; then he sat down at a table near the door. He was young, blond, and wiry-looking. Nobody seemed to notice his arrival.

"Just a little investigation," Bowdrie replied. "Hawkins knew that Pablo, Chiquita's friend, was one of the

Zaparo outfit. We're trying to learn all we can about Zaparo, and I'm curious as to how he knows."

The room was very still. Two Mexican cowhands who had been standing at the bar quietly left, and an older man with gray chin whiskers eased himself off his chair, and putting on his hat, went out a side door.

"Thought all of Zaparo's outfit were dead," Cassidy said.

"Looked like it," Bowdrie replied, "but it seems some of them were suspicious of Juan Pirón. They'd seen him talkin' with some gringos, and it didn't look good to them."

Cassidy shrugged. "Well, whatever, but don't hold him longer than you need to. We've got work to do."

The K-Bar boys left, mounted, and rode away. Bowdrie went to the bar and ordered a beer, turning the matter over in his mind. There was small chance the cowhand would talk, and a better-than-even chance he had nothing to tell. It might be nothing more than a cowhand going after a girl he believed might listen to him.

Bowdrie had an unhappy feeling that he was making a fool of himself. Certainly he would no longer be welcome at the K-Bar. Ranch hands were clannish, and a move against one of their number was a move against all. Yet he could not rid himself of the notion that he had a fingerhold on the problem.

Leaving his beer only half-finished, he went to his room, and was passing the spare room where he had left Hawkins when he heard a scurry of movement. Drawing his gun, he flung the door open and was just in time to see Hawkins going out the window. He grabbed for him with his left hand.

He caught the corner of a hip pocket and it ripped. The pocket tore away and something tinkled on the floor. Hawkins was out the window, sprawling on the ground. Scrambling to his feet, the bald-headed man started to run as Chick jumped through the window. As he hit the ground he thought he heard a low voice speaking to Hawkins; then a gun flashed and a bullet struck near him. Bowdrie fired in return at two indistinct riders. Two guns barked and a bullet nicked his arm, spoiling his last shot.

There was a pound of racing hooves, then silence. Moving with care, Bowdrie started toward where he had last seen Hawkins and saw the body of a man sprawled on the hard-packed earth in the pale, greenish light from the risen moon.

Waiting a moment, he listened but heard no sound. Kneeling, he struck a match.

The dead man was Hawkins. Hawkins had been wounded in the exchange of gunfire, but despairing of getting him away, somebody had put a gun to his head and blown his brains out.

Now men were coming from the cantina. Padilla and Pablo came up. Bowdrie motioned to the dead man and the obvious powder burns. "Looks like they killed him so he couldn't talk," he commented.

Which was foolish of them, for their actions spoke as loudly and clearly as anything Hawkins might have said. Their killing of him implied Hawkins would or might have had something to say. It pointed a finger at his killers and at the K-Bar.

Once in the spare room, Bowdrie lighted a candle and looked around. Something had fallen from Hawkins's pocket to the floor, but the first thing he found was the handcuffs. The lock had been opened either with a key or a lock-pick.

A gleam caught his eye, and on his knees, he retrieved a bright object from under the edge of the bed. It was a gold ring with an amethyst setting. It was a ring described in the list of loot stolen by Zaparo.

Hawkins, evidently thinking of Chiquita, had held out the ring as a gift to her for favors he hoped to receive. Obviously he had not known of her commitment to Pablo.

Chick slipped the ring into his pocket. He must work fast now. He crossed the patio on the run. The blond newcomer was at the bar. He turned as Bowdrie entered.

"Rip! How many came with you?"

"Deming an' Armstrong. Ain't that enough?"

"Get 'em an' come on! I'm headed for the K-Bar. If there's a fight this time, it will be something to write your girl about, believe me."

Once in the saddle, he let the roan have his head. The hammerhead outlaw knew when his master was in a hurry and he could set his own pace.

The K-Bar outfit might try to bluff it out or they might not even expect trouble. What he was hoping was that they would try to move the loot or get to where it was. The ranch itself was the logical place, of course, as it was one of the few places the mules could be taken without arousing suspicion or interest. Pack animals in such numbers do not just vanish from sight.

Rip Coker would be along with the two Rangers accompanying him. Bowdrie had spotted him the moment he entered the cantina, and realized McNelly had sent them along to help.

When he drew near the K-Bar he slowed the roan to a walk, keeping to the soft shoulder of the road, hoping a hoof would not strike stone. The other Rangers were not far behind, but speed was of first importance.

There was activity near a stack of hay, and some mules with packsaddles were being loaded. Three men were in sight as he approached, and he could hear cursing. There were lights on in the house. Was Katch involved too? Or was it only the ranch hands?

Chick Bowdrie stepped down from his horse. "You stand," he warned, "but if I yell, come a-runnin'."

The roan was already dozing, accustomed to such moments but prepared to take what rest he could get.

The other Rangers closed in and Bowdrie explained what he had in mind and then moved off, stepping softly and hoping his spurs would not jingle.

When he reached the back of the well-house, he took a quick glance about, then walked across to the back door of the ranch house. He had been in the house too many times before not to know his way. He crossed the kitchen, hearing a murmur of voices from the living room.

Walking softly behind the chairs in the big dining room, he reached the door and paused to listen. The door stood open but he was well back and out of sight.

"Forget it, Cassidy!" Katch was saying. "You're jumpy! If Hawkins is dead, he can't talk. That fool Ranger will think one of his own shots killed him. He likes to believe he's good with a six-shooter."

"Maybe you're right," Cassidy replied doubtfully, "but maybe he knows too much. After all, he knew about Pirón. How could he find out about him?"

"Don't get the wind up," Katch replied carelessly. "This is foolproof."

Katch got up and stretched. In the dim light he looked enormous.

"I told the boys to load the stuff so's we could move it," Cassidy said.

Katch brought his arms down slowly. "You *what*?" His tone was low but there was something so deadly in it that Bowdrie felt his scalp tighten.

"It seemed the thing to do. If they search the place, they'll find nothing."

Katch's tone was mild. "Ferd, if they did search, they'd never think to look in that haystack. Besides, the Rangers know me. I'm their friend. If that loot starts paradin' around in the moonlight, somebody is sure enough goin' to see it."

Cassidy had his hands flat on the table. "I'll go tell 'em to put it back," he said. "I guess I acted too fast."

"That's your trouble, Ferd. You're too jumpy. I don't like men who get jumpy, Ferd. You're a good man on a job, smooth as silk and cold as ice, but when we ain't workin' you're too easy to upset. Besides, I don't like men who give orders without consultin' me."

"I'm right sorry," Cassidy said. "You ain't mad, are you, boss?"

His features were sallow in the dim light, and suddenly Bowdrie knew what was about to happen. Big

Tom Katch was playing with his lieutenant as a cat plays with a mouse. Katch knew that Cassidy was on edge. He led him on now, building him to a crisis.

"No, I'm not mad, Ferd. Not mad at all." Katch smiled. "I just don't need you anymore, Ferd."

The words fell softly in the room and for a moment there was utter silence as the words sank into Ferd Cassidy's brain. Realization hit him like a blow. His eyes seemed to flare and he went for his gun. And Tom Katch shot him.

He had held the gun at his side, turned half away, so Ferd Cassidy, expecting no trouble here, had not even noticed.

Bowdrie stepped softly into the room, so softly that Tom Katch did not hear it. The big man was staring at the dying Cassidy with amused contempt. Katch holstered his gun.

Then his eyes lifted and his peripheral vision seemed to catch a glimpse of Bowdrie. He turned his head.

Bowdrie saw the shock in Katch's eyes, then a slow smile. He had to admire the man, for it had taken only that instant to adjust to the changed situation.

"How are you, Chick? I've been havin' some trouble with my foreman, seems like. He and some of the boys been doin' some outside jobs I didn't know about."

"I don't buy it, Katch. You can't lay it on them alone. You're the boss here. Yours is the brain. From the beginning I knew there was something I should remember. Something that hung in the back of my mind trying to be remembered.

"It didn't come to me until I saw that those handcuffs had been opened with a lock-pick. Then I realized who Cassidy was. When I knew who he was, I knew who you were."

"Don't tell me I was on your Ranger list of wanted men. I never saw Texas until a few years back, and I've lived right here all that time."

"What about Missouri, Tennessee, Ohio, and Nebraska? Four big jobs, four clean jobs, except for one thing. The gent that saw you on the platform at the railroad station in Dodge City.

"It just happened that a little fat drummer was standin' there who had known you in Memphis. Big Tom Caughter, the smartest crook of them all, the man who never left a witness and always got away with the loot. Ferd Cassidy was Lonnie Webb, a Kansas boy with a gift for picking locks, other people's locks."

Katch was thinking. Bowdrie could almost see his mind working, and this was a shrewd, dangerous man. Always before he had gotten away with it. No trail, no witnesses, no evidence. Four big jobs, and this was to be the fifth.

Katch shrugged. "Well, I guess a man can't win 'em all. With the money I've got cached I can be out in a couple of years."

"Sounds easy, doesn't it?" Bowdrie said. "But what about the killings?"

"You mean Zaparo? You can't prove I was there. As a matter of fact, I wasn't. Anyway, no jury is going to hang me for killing a few Mexican outlaws."

"I wasn't thinking of Zaparo. I was thinking of Ferd Cassidy. That was a cold-blooded killing. I saw it."

"Oh? So that's the way it is?" Katch eyed him with a steady, assured gaze. "Then we don't need a witness. When you die, who else will know?"

"The Rangers are outside waitin' for my signal," Bowdrie said. "Your boys are already rounded up, and without a shot fired. I was waiting to hear, but there never was a one. Now I'll take you."

Katch flashed a hand for his gun, incredibly fast, only Bowdrie was already shooting.

Coker stepped into the door. "Get 'em all?" Chick asked.

"Yeah." He looked at the bodies. "Both of them yours?"

"Only the big one." He looked at Katch and shook his head. "Rip, that man had brains, some education, and nerve. Why can't they ever realize they can't beat the law?"

Case Closed—No Prisoners

On the third day after the robbery, Sheriff Walt Borrow gave up and wired Austin. On the fifth day, late in the afternoon, a rider swung down at the hitch-rail in front of the saloon. Leaving the roan standing three-legged at the rail, he passed the saloon and went into the sheriff's office next door.

The rider was a young man, lean, and broad in the shoulders. Watchers glimpsed a hard brown face, wide at the cheekbones, a firm straight mouth, and a strong jaw. But it was the rider's eyes that stopped those who saw him face-on. They were intensely black, their gaze level and measuring. There was something about his eyes that made men uneasy, with a tendency to look quickly away.

"Looks like an Indian," Bishop commented. "Reminds me of Victorio, the Apache. I seen him once."

"I know him," Hardy Young said. "By sight, anyway. He's a Ranger from the Guadalupes."

Within the hour everybody within a radius of five miles knew that Ranger Chick Bowdrie was in town. What they did not know was that the saddle tramp who loafed in the Longhorn Saloon was Rip Coker, also a Texas Ranger.

Coker had drifted into town the day before, a grim, blond young man looking down-at-heel and broke. He let it be known that he was down to his last few dollars and ready for anything. With his horse for a stake he sat in a poker game and won enough for eating money. Most of the time he was just around, drinking a beer now and again and keeping his eyes and ears open.

The story of the robbery was being told around. Outlaws had hit the Bank of Kimble just before daylight to the tune of forty thousand dollars, and as Hardy Young commented to John Bishop, "That's a nice tune!"

Awakening as they did each morning, the townspeople had no idea what had taken place until Mary Phillips stopped Sheriff Borrow as he passed the Phillips home en route to breakfast and asked him to look for Josh.

"Ain't he to home, ma'am?" Borrow was mildly surprised. He had no idea that bankers got up so early.

"Somebody came to the door just before daylight and Josh answered it. He called back to me that he would be back in a minute, then he stepped out and I heard the door close. I dropped off to sleep and when I awakened he was still gone. That isn't like him."

Walt Borrow was undisturbed until he saw the bank's door ajar. Pushing it wider, he found Josh Phillips lying in a welter of gore, and the banker just managed to gasp out a few words before he died.

"Forced me!" he gasped, and lifted a hand horribly blackened by fire. "Threatened to burn . . . Mary, too!"

A question from Borrow elicited a few more words.

"Strangers! A . . . hawk . . ." His voice broke and he struggled for words. "Red!"

The town was enraged, but the rage was tempered by wonder, for there were no tracks, and nobody seemed to have seen anything. The outlaws had come and gone unseen, unheard. Only the body of Josh Phillips, the safe they forced him to open, and the forty thousand missing dollars proved their visit.

Stabling his horse in the livery stable an hour after his arrival, Bowdrie seemed not to notice the saddle tramp currying his horse in the next stall.

"Forty thousand was the most money the bank had in four months." Coker spoke softly. "How does that sound?"

"Like somebody was tipped off," Bowdrie agreed. "Keep your ears open."

John Bishop intercepted Bowdrie as he was entering the hotel with his saddlebags. Bishop was a tall young man with a crisp dark beard and an attractive smile.

"I led the posse that hunted for tracks," he said. "I'd be glad to help in any way."

"You found nothing?"

Bishop had a fine-featured but strong face. He looked like a man who knew what he wanted and how to get it. "Nothing I could swear to. There was some wind that night, and blown sand would make the tracks look older."

Bowdrie thanked him and went into the hotel. He wore a black flat-crowned, flat-brimmed hat, a black silk neckerchief, gray wool shirt, and black broadcloth trousers over hand-tooled boots with California spurs. His two guns were carried low and tied down, a style rarely seen. His eyes, as they slanted across the street, missed nothing.

Leaving his saddlebags in his room on the second floor, he returned to the lobby and passed through the connecting door into the restaurant adjoining. Only two tables were occupied, the nearest one by a man wearing a black suit, his hair plastered down on a round skull and parted carefully. His face was brick-red, his eyes a hard blue.

The girl who waited on Chick had red hair and a wide, friendly smile. She put down a cup of coffee in front of him.

"I always bring coffee to a rider," she said. "My pop taught me that."

"He must have been a wise man as well as an Irishman," Bowdrie said. "May I ask your name?"

"Ellen. And you are right about the Irish. My other name is Collins. My father was a sergeant in the cavalry."

A shadow loomed over the table. The big man in the black suit stood there, a napkin tucked under his chin, a cup of coffee in his hand.

"Howdy, suh! Mind if I join you?" Without waiting for a reply, he seated himself. "Name's Hardy Young. Cattle buyer. Ain't so young as I used to be, but just as hardy!"

He laughed loudly, then leaned over and whispered hoarsely, rolling his eyes from side to side as if to see who might be listening.

"Heard you was in town, suh! Frightful thing! Frightful! Always aim to help the law, that's what I say! Now, if there's anything you want looked into, you just ask Hardy Young! I know ever'body hereabouts!"

Bowdrie measured him for a cool half-minute before replying, and the hard blue eyes became uneasy. Hastily the man gulped a swallow of coffee.

"Thanks," Bowdrie replied. "This job will not take long."

Young stared, momentarily taken aback.

"None of them are very complicated," Bowdrie replied. "The ones planned so carefully are often the easiest. This case doesn't appear to be as difficult as many we get."

Hardy Young mopped his mustache with the back of his hand and sucked his teeth noisily. The blue eyes were round and astonished.

"That sounds like a Ranger!" he said. "It surely does!"

Bowdrie was irritated. He was nowhere near as confident as he sounded, but the man angered him. Yet he knew that once a job was complete, thieves were always somewhat worried. Had they been seen, after all? Had they forgotten some vital thing? In a robbery so carefully planned, the planner might have overlooked something. Hardy Young was obviously a busybody and a talkative man. If he repeated what Bowdrie had said, it might lead the thieves into some impulsive act.

If they acted suddenly, they might betray themselves, and without doubt they had a spy in the town. Somebody had informed them of the amount of money in the bank.

"Then you figure to close this case right up?"

Bowdrie shrugged. "No great rush. This is a nice little town and as soon as I report back to Austin they'll give me another job, maybe tougher than this.

"This case won't be tough. Their boss forgot one important item, and it will hang them all."

"*Hang* them?" Young looked startled.

"Phillips was killed, wasn't he? We'll hang them all—except," he added, "the man who gives us information. He'll get off easy."

Young clutched his knife and fork desperately. The food he had ordered brought to Bowdrie's table lay untouched before him.

He leaned forward. "There is such a man, then? You already know such a man?"

Purposely Bowdrie hesitated. "If there isn't," he said, "there will be. There's always one man who wants to dodge the noose."

After Young had left the table, Bowdrie lingered over his coffee. Something about the man disturbed him. At first he had believed him an irritating busybody; now he was not so sure.

Despite his comments to Young, Bowdrie had literally nothing upon which to work. Bishop had found no tracks, but as suggested, the wind might have wiped them out. Phillips's last words seems to imply the outlaws were strangers, and then there were his incomprehensible words about a "hawk . . . red."

The thieves had known when to strike and their clean escape seemed to indicate that they had covered the distance to their hideout under cover of darkness.

There seemed no answer to that, unless . . . It came to him with shocking suddenness. Unless they never left town at all!

Strangers, Phillips had said, and in a town the size of Kimble the banker would know everyone, and Sheriff Borrow had told him there were no strangers in town but the saddle tramp called Rip who had arrived after the robbery.

Ellen returned to his table with the coffeepot and sat down opposite him. "You should be careful," she warned. "Men who would rob a bank and torture a man as they did Mr. Phillips would stop at nothing."

"Thanks." He glanced at her thoughtfully. "You must see everything and hear everything in here. Have there been any strangers in town? They all come here to eat, don't they?"

"No, not all. But there was a man . . . I used to see him around San Antone when I was a little girl. His name was Latham, I think. He was here, but I saw him only once."

"What became of him? Did he have a horse?"

"I don't think so. He walked along the street, then he stopped outside and smoked a cigarette. After that he went around the corner and down the alley. I did not see him again."

Bowdrie's dark features revealed nothing, but his heart was pounding. This might be the first break.

Latham, the man she had seen, could have been Jack Latham, one of the Decker gang of outlaws.

Standing in front of the restaurant, he would have had a good chance to study the bank. Yet he had been on foot and he did not disappear in the direction of the livery stable or the town corral. Behind the double row of business buildings that faced Main Street there were only dwellings. If Latham had turned down an alley it could only have been to go to one of them.

Jack Latham was on the Fugitives List as a cattle rustler, a horse thief and killer. He was known to have worked with Comanche George Cobb and Pony Decker.

Ellen was right, of course. Such men would stop at nothing. They were utterly ruthless, dangerous men. Yet this robbery was unlike them. Behind this one was a different kind of intelligence, someone with new techniques, a new approach.

He talked for a while to Ellen, simply the casual

conversation of the town, the restaurant, the people. He learned nothing new but did acquire some knowledge of the community, its thinking, and its ways.

Returning to his room, Chick dropped on the edge of the bed and pulled off his boots. Then he sat very still, thinking.

And in the stillness of the unlit room he heard a movement.

His eyes went left, then right. Nothing. The hair prickled on his scalp and then he felt rather than heard a stealthy movement.

He sprang from the bed and turned swiftly, gun in hand. The rising moon illumined the room, but he could see nothing. It was empty, ghostly in the moonlight.

Once more he glanced around the room; then very cautiously he lighted a lamp. He had started to move away when he detected a faint movement among the blankets on the bed. Gun in hand, he reached with careful fingers and jerked the blanket back.

There, in a tight, deadly S, lay a sidewinder, one of the deadliest of desert rattlesnakes, a snake that does not coil but simply draws back its head and strikes repeatedly.

The snake's gaze was steady, unblinking. Man and reptile watched each other with deadly intensity. The room was on the second floor and the chance that such a snake had come there of its own choice was next to impossible.

Moving carefully, Bowdrie got a broom left standing in a corner, and a broken bed slat standing beside it. Using them as pincers, he lifted the snake and dropped it from the window. He heard the soft *plop* when it hit the ground.

After a careful examination of the room he undressed, got into bed, and went to sleep. He slept soundly and comfortably.

The sun was chinning itself on the eastern mountains when he awakened. His door was opening softly, stealthily. A big, carefully combed head was thrust into the room. Hardy Young found himself staring into the business end of a Colt.

"Stopped by t'see if you was havin' breakfast! I'm a-treatin', such! I was tryin' to be careful so's if you was still asleep I'd not wake you up."

The blue eyes roamed uneasily over the room. Chick sat up and reached for his pants with his left hand. "Mighty kind of you." He invited, "Come in an' set. I'll get dressed."

Young was manifestly uneasy and kept looking around as Chick dressed. "Sit down on the bed," Bowdrie suggested. "It's more comfortable."

He slung on his gunbelts and dropped the free gun into its holster. As he did so, he brushed lightly against Young, enough to make him stagger and drop to the bed.

His face gray, Young bounded to his feet as if stabbed. Bowdrie smiled pleasantly. "What's the matter, Hardy? Scared of something? You needn't be. I threw it out of the window."

"Threw what out?" Young blustered. "I got no idea what you're talkin' about."

The man's guilt was manifest and Bowdrie gripped the front of his stiff collar and twisted hard. His fingers were inside the collar and as his hand turned, his fist pressed against Young's Adam's apple. He shoved Young hard against the wall, still twisting.

The man's eyes bulged, he gasped for breath, and his face began to turn blue. Bowdrie slowly relaxed his grip, letting Young catch his breath. Then with his free hand he slapped Young across the face.

"Who's in this with you, Young? Talk, or I'll skin you alive!"

Bowdrie relaxed his grip a bit more. Gasping hoarsely, the big man said, "I don't know what you're talkin' about! Honest, I don't!"

Bowdrie jerked him away from the wall and kicked him behind the knees, and let go. Hardy Young hit the floor with a crash that shook the building.

"You'd better talk while you can. If you don't, Latham or one of the others will!"

Young's hand was at his throat but at the mention of Latham's name a kind of panic went through him. Bowdrie could almost see the man's mind working. If Bowdrie knew about Latham, how much more did he know?

"Get up!" Bowdrie said. "Get up an' get out! You've got until four this afternoon to talk. After that you hang with the rest of them!"

He was pushing his luck, he knew, but he had a feeling that Hardy Young was genuinely frightened. If the man would talk, it would save time, much time. Had the snake been Hardy's own idea? Or had somebody else done it or put Hardy up to doing it?

By riding Young, he might force them into a revealing move. When such men moved suddenly, they often made mistakes. Obviously somebody was worried or they would not have tried to get him killed by a rattler. Undoubtedly they believed he knew more than he did, which had been nothing.

Following a hurried breakfast, Bowdrie saddled the roan and rode out of town. His theory of the previous day, that the outlaws were still in Kimble, was still valid. Yet it would be impossible for a group of men to remain hidden for long in such a small town. Certainly there could not have been sufficient food for more than a few days, and he suspected they had already been in town longer than planned.

Drawing rein under some trees on the slope near the edge of town, Bowdrie sat his saddle, studying the place. His view was a good one, and as he studied the layout his eyes turned again and again to a large ranch house almost hidden in a grove of cottonwoods.

A huge barn, several corrals, various outbuildings. The barn backed up to an arroyo that wound through the low hills on the edge of town.

It was very hot now and the air was breathless. Chick mopped his face and neck. Squinting against the glare, he used the trees as a screen and rode down, crossed the trail, and entered the arroyo. He found no tracks and scowled with disappointment.

Yet he knew no track could long endure in this sand.

He was riding along immersed in thought, and the sharp jerk at his shoulder almost failed to register until he heard the metallic slam of the gunshot.

A frail tendril of smoke lifted from a rocky knoll, and touching a spur to the roan's ribs, Bowdrie sent him up out of the arroyo and on a dead run for the knoll itself. Another rifle shot rang out but the bullet missed, and the roan went charging up the knoll. Bowdrie's gun was in his hand, but the knoll was empty!

Amazed and angry, he took a quick swing around among the rocks. If the shot had come from here, the marksman was gone.

Perplexed, he looked all around. The grass was disturbed but he found no distinguishable tracks. Horses and cattle had been on the knoll, and there was a confusion of tracks, scratches, and scuffed earth.

His shoulder was smarting by the time he reached town. The shot had merely split the fabric of his shirt and scraped the skin.

He swung down at the livery stable and glanced over at the two or three loafers. "Anybody want to make a half-dollar caring for a horse?"

Rip Coker was seated on a box. "How about me? They cleaned me at poker, and a half a dollar would buy me a couple of meals."

They walked into the barn, Bowdrie giving instructions.

"Who owns the big house over by the wash?" he asked when they were alone.

"I thought of it, but that's the Bishop place. He's well off, and one of the leading citizens. He and his brother put up money to help build both the church and the school. John Bishop is the mayor."

"What's his brother do?"

"Red? He ranches down in Mexico. He's never here, and hasn't even been here so far as I know, even though the Bishops sort of regard this as their town, and always contribute to worthy causes."

Bowdrie outlined all that had happened and what little he had learned, adding what Ellen had told him about Latham.

"Sounds like him. From all I hear, that banker looked like a Comanche had worked on him. He was badly used."

Ellen came immediately to his table when Bowdrie seated himself in the restaurant a few minutes later. "Does Sheriff Borrow eat here?" he asked.

"He was in, looking for you, perhaps an hour ago. It might have been two hours. I've been pretty busy until now."

"Thanks. If he doesn't come in, I'll look him up."

The outer door opened and when he glanced up, the newcomer turned out to be John Bishop.

"Any luck, Bowdrie?" His eyes went to Chick's shoulder. "Don't tell me you've been shot?"

"I didn't tell you," Bowdrie said sharply. "It seems you're a good guesser. From where you stand, that could be a thorn scratch or a barbed-wire cut, but if you'd like to believe it was a shot, you've the choice."

"You seem to be touchy. Is the case getting on your nerves?"

"Of course not. You haven't been a Ranger, Bishop. Most cases are routine. All a man needs is a little time and patience. All this case needed was a fresh viewpoint. It's like I told Hardy Young, the boss in a case like this always overlooks something. That's a beginning. Then somebody gets scared and they talk so they won't have to hang like the rest of them."

"At least you're confident. That's more than Borrow can say."

"He doesn't know all that we know, and his experience in crime has been local. In the Rangers you run into everything. But even Young was surprised when I mentioned Jack Latham."

Without seeming to pay attention, Bowdrie was watching Bishop for a reaction. If there was any, it was well hidden.

Bishop's eyes were on him and Bowdrie felt a tide of recklessness welling up within him. He had no evidence at all, but regardless of what Coker had said of Bishop, that ranch was simply too well located for what had been happening. He pushed his luck.

"The well-planned crimes are often the simplest. A plan is a design like that of a weaver, and all you have to do is get hold of one of the threads and it all begins to unravel."

"And you've found the thread?"

Bishop's eyes reflected his skepticism, but under that lay something else. Apprehension, maybe?

"I've got two or three threads," Bowdrie said. "The trouble with well-planned crimes is that the planner is never content. He always wants to take another stitch here or there. The first thread was that this mysterious crime was simply too mysterious. It was overdone. Nobody saw anyone entering or leaving town and there were no tracks. The second thread was the hour of the crime and the way it was done.

"Then came the added touches. A snake in my bed that was intended to kill or scare me. The next touch was the shot somebody took at me, which indicates whoever did this crime is not sure of himself. Or somebody connected with it isn't sure.

"That was pure stupidity. I was sent alone on this job, but if I got killed you'd have a company of Rangers in here turning over every stone in town.

"It also proves what I suspected from the beginning: there were no tracks because the thieves never left town. They are here now, right in Kimble."

"That's absurd!" Bishop sounded angry. "This is a nice little town. Everybody knows everybody else. Why would they stay in a town with everybody hunting them? I was on the search myself and we found nobody."

"Exactly. Nobody thought of searching houses, merely of getting out on the trails. A thief would be running, so they would chase him. All the thieves had to do was sit tight, and with friends in town, that would be easy."

"Friends?"

"They had to have friends. Somebody had to tell them when there was enough money in the bank to make it worthwhile."

"That doesn't make sense," Bishop said. "I am afraid you're going off on a tangent."

"It makes a lot of sense," Bowdrie persisted. "Whoever pulled this job is outsmarting himself. That shot today, for example. As a miss it was very revealing."

"Revealing? How do you mean?"

"How does a man vanish off the face of the earth? I don't believe in magic, Bishop. I am a practical man."

Bishop shrugged. "I know nothing of crime, so I hope you find the guilty men. We've tried very hard to build a law-abiding community here. Sheriff Borrow and I worked out a plan to protect the town from just this sort of thing."

"It was a good setup," Bowdrie replied mildly. "Sheriff Borrow told me about it."

"We've tried very hard to build a good community here. That's why we all contributed to the church and the school."

"That makes sense." Bowdrie smiled. "A good community is a prosperous one. One with money around."

John Bishop threw him a sharp glance, as if trying to see meaning behind the comment. Bowdrie's expression was innocent.

"You're ranching yourself, are you not?" Bowdrie inquired. "Horse ranching, I think? I've noticed some fine horses around town, some with plenty of speed."

Bishop did not reply. His fingers gripped the cup Ellen had brought him.

"By the way," Bowdrie continued. "What's Red doing now?"

The fingers on the cup tightened. Bishop looked up, and the pretended friendliness was gone from his eyes.

"He's ranching in Sonora." Bishop pushed back his chair. "I'll see you later."

He stood up and turned to go, but Chick's voice stopped him. "By the way . . ." Bowdrie's tone was gentle. "Don't leave town and tell your brother not to."

Bishop turned sharply around. "What do you mean by that? I told you . . ." He paused, gaining control of himself. "I am beginning to see what you have in mind, but it won't work, Bowdrie. Don't try to frame me or my brother."

Bowdrie got up and stepped past him to the counter where Ellen was standing. "Let me treat Mr. Bishop," he said cheerfully. "I enjoy doing it. In fact, I plan to arrange for all his meals . . . as long as he will need them!"

"Don't start anything you can't finish!" Bishop's eyes were mean. "I am a friend of the governor!"

Bowdrie smiled. "Perhaps, but is he your friend?"

Bishop slammed the door and Chick smiled at Ellen. "You know, I always did like a girl with freckles on her nose!"

He walked outside and glanced along the street. He was displeased with himself. He had not intended to push Bishop so far, although in his own mind he was sure he was merely a smooth crook. Under the guise of being a public-spirited citizen he could have planned and pulled off this robbery without being suspected. What the case had needed was a fresh viewpoint, someone from outside the town, unimpressed by Bishop.

The worst of it was that Bowdrie had pushed too far without a bit of proof. He was sure that Bishop and his brother had engineered the robbery and killed Josh Phillips. Moreover, he was sure they had tried to kill him, but he could prove nothing. Yet Bishop was worried; that much was obvious.

Coker was loafing in front of the saloon. "Get on your horse and light out of here," Chick advised. "The first telegraph station you hit, wire to McNelly. Ask him to come runnin'."

"You've been talkin' to Bishop?"

"He's our man, I'm sure of it."

"I've been thinkin'. It's possible. Nobody would notice extry horses over there, nor a few extry men around. He carries a stock of grub and he's the only place aside from the restaurant which could feed men for more than a day or two."

"I'm going to see Borrow, but you'd better get out fast. I've a hunch my talk with Bishop will blow the lid off. He's supposed to be smart, but doesn't have sense enough to just sit tight."

The sheriff's office door was closed, but Bowdrie turned the knob and stepped in. He stopped, the door half-closed behind him. Just beyond the corner of the desk and inside the bedroom door Bowdrie saw a pair of boot toes turned up.

He sprang past the desk and stopped with his hands on the doorjamb. On the floor, lying on his back, was Sheriff Walt Borrow, the manner of his death obvious. Under his breastbone was the haft of a knife.

Bowdrie stopped and touched the dead man's hand. It was cold. He straightened up and glanced around. The picture became clear when he saw the chair in the shadows near several coats hung from a clothes tree.

Crossing to the chair, Bowdrie seated himself. He was facing the doors but well back in the shadows. Whoever sat in the chair would see whoever came in from the street, but Borrow, coming in from the glare of the sun, would not have seen his killer.

Near the chair were three cigarette butts, lying where the killer had dropped them. Borrow, as did most men of the time and the area, smoked cigars. Cigarettes were a Mexican custom only beginning to cross the border, so these might have been smoked by someone living south of the border.

Here the killer had waited. There was no evidence of struggle, and Borrow had been a strong, tough man. The killer might have struck from his chair, but it was likely that he had risen as Borrow drew close and driven the knife upward to the heart. Soundless, abrupt, and final.

But why?

Bowdrie recalled the old man's kindly features at their first meeting. "I'm stumped," Borrow confessed. "The answer keeps naggin' at me. It's right on the trail edge of my thinkin', but I can't quite get it out into the open."

He had glanced at the blanket roll Chick was carrying. "Might's well leave that here. You won't need it at the hotel."

And the tight roll of his poncho and blankets still stood in the corner where he had left it, yet the roll was neither as tight nor was it rolled in quite the same way now. Why would Borrow, or anyone, open his blanket roll?

Dropping to his knees, he pulled the roll loose. As it opened, a fold of paper fell out. Taking it up, Bowdrie opened it for a quick look. It was all he needed. Instantly he was on his feet.

Hurriedly bundling the roll together, he tossed it into a corner. The door opened almost in his face, and Ellen, the freckles dark against the paleness of her face, stood there.

"Oh, Mr. Bowdrie! Please be careful! They're after you!"

"Who is?"

"They were talking out in back of the restaurant. They did not guess anyone was around. One of the men said they would get you when you left the office."

"Then they saw you come to the door. That's bad, Ellen!"

"I thought of that. If they ask, I'll tell them you forgot to pay for your meal and I came after you."

"Good!" He reached into his pocket and counted out some money. "There! That'll pay for what I ate and the next two meals, if I should forget again."

He put the money in her hand. "Now, do something for me. If you see that lantern-jawed blond drifter they call Rip, get to him and tell him what is happening. Tell him where I am but not to come here. Understand?"

She turned away quickly, clutching the money in her hand. She paused an instant, flashing him a quick, frightened smile. "Good luck, Chick!"

He listened to the click of her heels on the walk, hoping she would not be stopped. He watched her enter the restaurant, from which she would be able to watch the trail into town.

They would not wait long now. If he did not appear on the street, they would come here. They had proved themselves to be impatient men. Somehow they had discovered the sheriff had finally found the solution and had killed him. Now they must kill Bowdrie.

Chick took stock of his position. The sheriff's office was separated from the saloon by a gap of about thirty feet. On the other side there was nothing but an open slope.

The building comprised four rooms. Two solidly built cells on one side of a narrow hall, on the other the office itself, and farther along, the sheriff's living quarters.

Bending over the dead man, he removed his gunbelt and pistol. The pistol was fully loaded. From the gun rack he got down the sheriff's old Sharps and his Spencer as well as a double-barreled shotgun. From a drawer he took ammunition for these guns and arranged it in neat rows on the desk.

Then he took up the body and carried it to the bed, where he straightened it out and covered it with a blanket.

Bowdrie knew that in this situation he could not depend on Rip Coker. The Ranger would go through hell and high water to do his duty, but the telegraph operator might be a friend of the Bishops or of Young. He would undoubtedly send his message both to McNelly and to Major Jones, who was actually in charge in this area.

The wise course was to depend on neither. The problem was his, to be solved here and now. Even if the message got through, there was small chance they would arrive in time. If they did, an arrest might be made without a fight through sheer numbers, but considering the type of men he was facing, even that was doubtful. Chick Bowdrie preferred to make arrests without trouble, but such occasions were rare in a land where the border was so near, escape so possible.

Undoubtedly the robbery had been pulled off by Red Bishop and the Decker-Latham outfit. John Bishop and Hardy Young had no doubt planned it, knowing of the money in the bank and choosing the time. Riders would attract no attention on Bishop's ranch, and there was plenty of cover for going and coming.

Due to the sheriff's recollection, Bowdrie knew how the bandits had arrived as well as where the shot came from that was meant to kill him.

The afternoon was warm and still. No breath of wind stirred the thick dust in the long, hot street. The false-fronted buildings across the street looked parched and gray.

Bowdrie mopped sweat from his face, loosened his neckerchief, then sat down behind the desk. There was a bucket of water in the shadowed bedroom, but no food.

Food did not worry him. This fight would be history before he had a chance to be hungry again.

He hoped to kill no one, but he was alone against five or six desperate men who had shown their style in torturing Phillips.

Nor could he expect help from the town. None of them would believe Bishop was a thief. Nor did they know Borrow was murdered. There was a pot of coffee on the stove. Hot though it was outside, he poured a cup. It was strong and bitter, but he liked it.

Down the street he heard a few steps on the board-walk, then silence. Well, if he got himself killed, he had no family to worry about it. He was a loner. His family was the Rangers, his world was his job.

Ellen . . . now there was a likely lass. But even if she

were interested in him, how could he ask any girl to
marry a man who might end up on a slab at any moment?
Still, a lot of the Rangers were married, and happily,
too.

Bowdrie walked back to the cells, and keeping his
head from in front of the small window, he peered out.
There was a pile of scrap lumber back there, and watching it, he saw the grass stir. So they had a man out
there, too.

He walked back to the office, and at that moment
Bishop called out, "Bowdrie? Step over here a minute,
will you? I've got something to show you."

"Bring it over here, John," Chick called back. "I'm
not going to make it that easy for you."

He was impatient for them to get on with it. He had
lain for hours without moving when stalking someone,
but when the chips were down, he disliked waiting.

"Whoever fired that shot from the rocks gave you
away, John!" he called out. "I know all about that old
watercourse now!"

Somebody swore and Bishop stepped back out of
sight. Then there was silence.

Bishop was handling this all wrong. He had the total
sympathy of the townspeople, but now they would begin to wonder. Why was John Bishop, their mayor and
leading citizen, trying to kill a Texas Ranger? Bowdrie
had yelled, hoping others would be listening, and wondering now.

In the midst of the stillness Bowdrie had a sudden
inspiration. Taking a couple of rawhide riatas Borrow
had hanging on the clothes tree, he knotted one over a
nail over the door to the bedroom, and crawling across
the floor, knotted the other end over a nail near the
outside door.

Crawling back, he took a turn around the doorknob,
rigging a crude pulley. Then he fastened the end of his
riata through an armhole of Borrow's poncho in such a
way that by pulling on the riata he could make it move
by the window. The light was such that anyone outside

would see movement but could not detect who or what it was unless standing right outside.

He pulled the poncho opposite the window, then pulled again. Instantly the poncho jerked and a rifle bellowed. Bowdrie was watching, and when the rifle flashed, he fired.

There was a crash of glass and a startled yelp. If he hadn't hit somebody, he had at least scared him. His shot was followed by a scattered volley that broke much of the front window.

Keeping the Spencer in his hands, Bowdrie waited. Sweat trickled down his chest under his shirt. He wiped his hands on his pants. A searching shot struck the wall over his head, but he knew they could not see him, although given time, they might figure out his position. Bishop and Young must both have seen the inside of this office many times.

He refilled his cup, sipped coffee, and sat back in his chair, waiting. He had two front windows and a side window, and the glass in the front windows was more than half gone. By now the people around town were wondering just what was going on.

He waited, not wanting to waste a shot and hoping they would believe he had been hit.

Nothing happened. Chick yawned. If they waited long enough, the Rangers would be here. Of course, they could not know that. Yet even if he left the office somehow he was handicapped in not knowing the men he was fighting.

A shot rang out and a bullet cut a furrow in the desk and buried itself in the wall. Another struck the floor and ventilated the wastebasket. They were probing with fingers of lead.

He reached for his cup and caught a glimpse of movement from the window on the second floor of the harness shop across the street. There was a curtain inside that window, but he could detect a reflection of movement.

A man was inching his way along the rooftop to fire

from behind the false front of the building next to the harness shop and directly opposite. The man was getting into position to fire down into the office. He was out of sight behind the false front but dimly reflected in the window over the harness shop.

Bowdrie took a swallow of coffee, put the cup down, and took the Spencer from his lap. He studied the window and then the roof. Taking up the Spencer, he took careful aim, drew in a breath, and let it out slowly and then squeezed off his shot.

The heavy rifle leaped in his hands, firing right into the false front of the building. A pistol bullet would penetrate several inches of pine at that distance, and the .56-caliber Spencer would not be impeded by the half-inch boards on the front opposite.

He heard a rifle clatter and fall into the dirt; then a man slid to the roof edge, clawing madly to keep from sliding on the steep roof, then falling.

The man scrambled up, obviously hurt but moving. As he started to run, Bowdrie, with only the wide posterior for target, squeezed off another shot. There was an agonized yell and the man disappeared.

Bowdrie thumbed two shells into the Spencer, then hit the floor as a hail of bullets riddled the windows and the door. One bullet ripped through the desk, leaving a hole in a half-open drawer right in front of his face.

The shooting died down and he got up just in time to see a man sprinting across the street. Bowdrie fired and the runner drew suddenly to his tiptoes, then spilled over into the dust. "If you weren't one of them," Bowdrie said aloud, "you used damn poor judgment!"

He slipped down the hall to the back cell. There was still a man behind the lumber pile, but there was no chance for a shot.

Returning to the office, he stood well back in the room and searched the line of buildings opposite. He could see nothing.

He put down the Spencer, mopped his face, and reached for the gun. Dust stirred on the floor and he wheeled, his grasp closing on the shotgun. Comanche George Cobb stood in the side door, his pistol in his hand.

Bowdrie saw the man's eyes blaze, and the pistol thrust forward; he saw the man's thumb bend as it pulled the hammer back, and Bowdrie squeezed both triggers on the shotgun.

Cobb's body jerked as if kicked by a mule, and he took a staggering step backward before he fell, a spur hooking itself on the doorjamb.

"Two gone," he muttered, "and maybe one wounded."

He started to move, then froze in mid-stride as his nostrils caught the faintest smell of smoke.

Smoke, and then the crackle of flames!

Grabbing up shotgun shells, he jammed them into his pockets; then he reloaded the shotgun itself. Testing the sheriff's pistols for balance, he thrust them into his waistband.

Flames crackled outside and smoke began to curl up from the floor and into the windows. Evidently they had gotten under the building and set fire to it.

Outside, men waited to cut him down the minute he showed himself. He might get some of them, but they would surely get him.

Suddenly he remembered something seen earlier. He glanced up. A trapdoor to the loft over the office. Now, if there was only a second trapdoor to the roof, as was often the case when access was left for possible repairs . . .

Leaping atop the desk, he shoved the trap aside, and grasping the lip of the opening, he pulled himself up. Though smoke was gathering even there, Bowdrie made out the square framework of a trapdoor in the roof. Closing the trapdoor behind him, he raced along the joists, shotgun in hand, unfastened the hasp, and lifted himself to the flat roof.

The rooftop slanted down slightly to allow rain to run off. Bowdrie looked over the edge. There was no one in sight, as they evidently believed Comanche George was still there.

Swinging his legs over, he hung for a minute, then dropped, knees bent to absorb the shock. He hit the ground, staggered, recovered, looked quickly around, his shotgun poised for firing.

There was nobody in sight.

A quick dash and he was behind the Longhorn Saloon. Opening the back door, he stepped in. A half-dozen men stood near the wide front window, watching the street. Opposite, plainly visible in the window across the street, was John Bishop.

The bartender turned his head, and when he saw Bowdrie, his face paled. He drew back, his hands falling to his sides.

Bowdrie walked quickly to the front door. The fire destroying the sheriff's office could be plainly heard.

"Hope it don't burn the whole town!" somebody commented.

"What started Bishop on a rampage? Who're those fellers with him?"

"Don't know any of 'em. Strangers. Somebody said that Ranger killed Walt Borrow."

The roof of the building collapsed suddenly, and John Bishop stepped into the street, a red-haired man beside him. From down the street Hardy Young was approaching.

"Stand aside, men!" Bowdrie said, and as they turned, he said quietly, "Red Bishop robbed your bank. John Bishop murdered Borrow because your sheriff had found him out. The dead man out there is Jack Latham, the outlaw. Keep out of this!"

He stepped into the street as Hardy Young came up to the Bishops. Where was Decker, the man Bowdrie had shot when he fell from the roof?

Bowdrie stepped off the walk. "Bishop! I arrest you for robbing the Bank of Kimble, for the murders of Josh Phillips and Walt Borrow!"

The three men turned, staring as if at a ghost. John Bishop had an instant of panic. "How in . . . !"

"Drop your guns. You will get a fair trial!"

"Trial, hell!" Red Bishop's gun started to lift, and Bowdrie fired the shotgun. One barrel, then the other. The group were close together, the distance no more than sixty feet.

Red Bishop was shooting when he took the shotgun blast. John Bishop caught a good half of a load of buckshot and toppled back against the hitching rail. He was fully conscious, fully aware.

Hardy Young was running away down the street. He was running, crazed with fear, when the horsemen rounded the corner into the street. He glimpsed them and tried to turn away, and they saw him and tried to rein in. Both were too late.

The charging horses ran him down and charged over his big body, trampling him into the dust.

Rip Coker was in the lead, McNelly right behind him. "Bowdrie? You all right?"

Automatically Bowdrie extracted the shells and reloaded the shotgun. "All right," he said. "Case closed—no prisoners."

"Where's Cobb? And Decker?"

Bowdrie explained in as few words as possible. "Borrow finally figured it out. There's a draw comes in from the south on Bishop's land. Riders could come right up from Mexico, then follow that draw right to his ranch. Nobody need see them at all.

"Once you forgot who Bishop was and just looked at the situation, it almost had to be him. Borrow left a note in my bedroll just in case. He should have the credit for this one.

"I think," Bowdrie added, "you'll find the bank's money in Bishop's house. If they aren't carrying it on their bodies."

"Good job, Bowdrie!" McNelly said. "Thanks!"

Bowdrie lifted a hand. "There's coffee waitin' for me inside. Come an' join me, if you're of a mind to."

He turned toward the restaurant, suddenly tired. It was cool inside, and Ellen was standing by a table with the coffeepot in hand.

Someday, he thought, someday he might find a town like this, a place where he could stop, get acquainted, and build something.

"Your family will be glad you're safe," Ellen said.

"I've got no family," he replied. "I've got nobody. Only the Rangers and a mean roan horse. That's all I got. Maybe it's all I'll ever have."

As he sat down, she was pouring his coffee, and he *was* tired. Very tired.

HISTORICAL NOTE:

THE BUFFALO WALLOW FIGHT

It was September 10, 1874, and a party of six—two scouts and four soldiers—carrying dispatches from their camp on McClellan Creek, had started for Camp Supply in Indian Territory. The group consisted of Billy Dixon and Amos Chapman, scouts, accompanied by Sergeant Woodhall and Privates Smith, Rath, and Harrington.

At sunrise on the morning of the twelfth they were attacked by a war party of approximately 125 Kiowa and Comanche Indians. The attack came at a point between Gageby Creek and the Washita River, about eighteen miles from where the Texas town of Canadian now stands.

In the bitter fight that followed, four of the men were wounded before noon, one of them fatally. Billy Dixon discovered a buffalo wallow some distance away and ran for it. He was wounded in the process but dropped into the comparative shelter of the wallow and called for the others to join him. He then ran back and helped one man who had a broken leg.

With their knives they built up an earthen parapet that offered a little more shelter. They had plenty of ammunition, but neither food nor water, and they suffered from the blazing heat.

All day the Indians maintained their attack, at times

sniping from cover, occasionally charging on horseback, sometimes circling about, but at all times keeping the pressure on the defenders.

Soon all six were wounded, and Private Smith, although dying, tried hard to help the defense.

A buffalo wallow, for those unaware of plains conditions at the time, was simply a place where buffaloes chose to wallow in the dust, just as a dog will. In so doing they usually rubbed out the grass in an area that might be fifteen feet in diameter. The spot might be in constant use for some time, and as a result there would be a small hollow that would offer some protection from enemy fire.

Late in the evening, as darkness was descending, a violent thunderstorm struck the area. The rain lashed the prairie with its fury, drenching both Indians and white men, but it brought life-saving water to the defenders. The rain not only quenched their thirst but left a small pool in the lowest part of the wallow.

Amos Chapman, Harrington, and Sergeant Woodhall were seriously wounded. Rath and Dixon, although wounded, were not disabled, and they continued to fight off the attackers. Both Chapman and Dixon were widely known frontiersmen, and Dixon was reputed to be one of the best rifle-shots in the West. Both were buffalo hunters, widely experienced in Plains warfare and undoubtedly known to the Indians who attacked them.

On the morning of the thirteenth, just before daylight, Dixon managed to slip away and make contact with an Army unit. The Indians fled, taking their wounded with them. Private Smith died and was buried in the buffalo wallow. Others of the party were recommended for decoration by General Nelson Miles.

Billy Dixon, of whom many stories could be told, was twenty-four years old at the time.

Down Sonora Way

Down on his stomach in the sand behind his dead horse, Chick Bowdrie waited for the sun to go down. It was a hot Sonora sun and the nearest shade was sixty yards away in a notch of the Sierra de Espuelas, where Tensleep Mooney waited with a Winchester.

Bowdrie had scooped out sand to dig himself a few inches deeper below the surface, but a bullet burn across the top of his shoulder and two double holes in his black flat-crowned hat demonstrated both the accuracy and the intent behind Tensleep's shooting.

Five hundred miles behind them in Texas were two dead men, the seventh and eighth on the list of Mooney's killings, and Bowdrie was showing an understandable reluctance to become number nine.

The sun was hot, Bowdrie's lips were cracked and dry, his canteen was empty. A patient buzzard circled overhead and a tiny lizard stared at the Ranger with wide, wondering eyes. It was twenty miles to water unless some remained in the *tinaja* where Mooney was holed up, and twenty miles in the desert can be an immeasurable distance.

Neither man held any illusions about the other. Tensleep Mooney was a fast hand with a six-shooter and an excellent rifle shot. His courage was without question. His feud with the gunslinging Baggs outfit was a legend in Texas. Al Baggs had stolen Mooney's horse. Mooney trailed him down, and in the gun battle that followed, killed him, recovering his horse. The Baggs family were Tennessee feudal stock and despite the fact that killing a horse thief was considered justifiable homicide, a brother and a cousin came hunting Tensleep. Mooney took two Baggs bullets and survived. The Baggs boys took three of Mooney's slugs and didn't.

From time to time a Baggs or two took a shot at Mooney, and at least two attempts were made to trap him. Others were killed and the last attempt resulted in a woman being shot. Then Tensleep unlimbered his guns and went to work. Until then he had been rolling with the punches but now he decided if the Baggs clan wanted war, they should have it.

Gene Baggs, the most noted gunslinger of the outfit, was in San Antonio. One Tuesday night Mooney showed up and gave Gene Baggs his chance. The Variety Theater rang with gunshots and Gene died of acute indigestion caused by absorbing too much lead on an empty stomach.

Killings seven and eight had taken place near Big Spring, one of them a Baggs, the other an itinerant gunfighting cattleman named Caspar Hanna. Settling disputes with guns was beginning to be frowned on in Texas, so the Rangers got their orders and Bowdrie got his.

Mooney was tricky and adept at covering his trail. Cunning as a wolf, he shook off his trailers and even lost Bowdrie on two occasions. Irritated, Bowdrie followed him to the Mexican border and kept on going. Out of his bailiwick though it was, the chase had now become a matter of professional and personal pride.

So now they were in the dead heart of Apache country, stalemated until darkness. If Mooney escaped in the dark, Bowdrie was scheduled to walk home, the odds against his survival a thousand to one. If one left out the heat and lack of water, even the miles of walking in boots meant for riding, there were always the Apaches.

"Thirsty, Ranger?" Mooney called.

"I'll drink when I'm ready," Bowdrie replied. "You want to come out with your hands up? You'll get a fair trial."

"I'd never live for the trial. Without my guns in Baggs country? I wouldn't last three days."

"Leave that to the Rangers."

"Much obliged. I'll leave it to Mooney."

Neither man spoke again and the hour dragged on. Bowdrie tried licking dry lips with a dry tongue. The heat where he lay was not less than one hundred and twenty degrees. Shifting his position drew a quick bullet. Carefully he began to dig again, trying to get at the rifle scabbard on the underside of his horse.

Bowdrie had nothing but respect for Mooney. Under any circumstances but the present the two might have worked a roundup together. Tensleep was a tough cowhand from the Wyoming country that gave him his name, a man who had started ranching on his own, a man who had been over the cow trails to Montana from Texas, who had fought Indians and rustlers.

Bowdrie continued to dig, finally loosening the girth on the dead horse.

"Somethin' out there." Mooney spoke suddenly, and Chick almost looked up, then cursed himself for a fool. It was a trap.

"Somebody travelin' north." Mooney's voice was just loud enough for Bowdrie to hear.

"In this country? You've got to be crazy."

He lay quiet, thinking. There had been no faking in Mooney's tone, and travelers in this country meant, nine times out of ten, Apaches. They were in the middle of an area controlled by Cochise, with his stronghold just to the north in New Mexico. If those were Apaches out there, they were in trouble.

Silence, and then Mooney spoke again, just loud enough for him to hear. "Somebody out there, all right. Can't quite make 'em out. Three or four riders, an' I'd say one was a woman."

A woman in this country? *Now?* Bowdrie wanted to chance a look, but if he lifted his head, Mooney might kill him.

"Walkin' their horses." Mooney was a trifle higher than Bowdrie and could see better.

Both men were hidden, Bowdrie by cactus and rock, Mooney by a notch of rocks that hid both himself and his horse.

"The man's hurt, got his arm in a sling, bandage on his head. Looks like the woman is holdin' him on his horse."

Bowdrie had dug deep enough to pull the girth loose, and now he pulled the saddle off and got at his Winchester. As he lifted the Winchester clear, it showed above the rocks.

"That won't do you no good, Bowdrie," Mooney said. "You lift your head to shoot an' I'll ventilate it."

"Leave that to me," Bowdrie replied cheerfully. "I'd rather take you in alive, because you'd keep better in this heat, but if I have to, I'll start shootin' at the rocks in back of you. The ricochets will chop you to mincemeat."

That, Mooney realized unhappily, was the plain, unvarnished truth. He rubbed a hand over his leather-brown face and narrowed his blue eyes against the sun's glare. He knew that Ranger out there, knew that behind that Apache-like face was as shrewd a fighting brain as he had ever known. No other man could have followed him this far. He peered through the rocks once more.

"Dust cloud." There was a silence while Bowdrie waited, listening. "Somebody chasin' the first bunch, I reckon. Quite a passel of 'em. The first bunch is comin' right close. Three horses, a man wounded bad, a woman an' two youngsters. The kids are ridin' double."

After a moment Mooney added, "Horses about all in. They've come fast an' hard."

"Comin' this way?"

"No, they'll pass us up."

A fly buzzed lazily in the hot afternoon sun and

Bowdrie could hear the sound of the approaching horses. Hidden as he and Mooney were, there was not a chance they'd be seen.

"Should be water at Ojo de Monte." The man's voice was ragged with exhaustion. "But that's twenty miles off."

"After that?"

"Los Mosquitos, or the Casa de Madera, another thirty miles as the crow flies. You'll have to keep to low ground. I'll try to hold 'em off from those rocks up ahead."

"No!" The woman's voice was strong. "No, George. If we're going to die, let it be together!"

"Don't be a fool, Hannah! Think of the children! You might get through, you might save them and yourself."

Chick Bowdrie shifted his body in the sand. A cloud of dust meant a good-sized bunch of Apaches. A small bunch would make no dust. And they were sure of their prey, for this was their country, far from any aid.

If they kept on after the man and his family, they would never see Mooney or Bowdrie. Bowdrie was realist enough to realize all they had to do was lie quiet. The Indians would not see their tracks, as they had come in from the north and the Apaches were coming from the west. Moreover, they would be too intent on their prey to look for other tracks.

"Mooney?" He spoke just loud enough for the outlaw to hear. "Are we goin' to stand for this? I say we call off our fight and move into this play."

"Just about to suggest the same thing, Ranger. Call 'em back."

Chick Bowdrie got to his feet. The family were moving away, but within easy hailing distance.

"Hey! Come back here! We'll help you!"

Startled, they drew up and turned to stare. "Come over here! I'm a Texas Ranger. You'd never make it the way you're headin'!"

They rounded their horses and walked them closer. The man's face was haggard, the bandage on his head was bloody. The youngsters, hollow-eyed and frightened, stared at them. The woman, not yet thirty, had a flicker of hope in her eyes.

"What we can offer ain't much better," Bowdrie said, "but two more rifles can help. If he tried to hold 'em off, they'd just cut around him an' have you all with no trouble."

"They'd get you before you could say Sam Houston. You get down an' come into the rocks." Tensleep paused, grinning at Bowdrie. "But not where that in-curvin' rock is." He rolled his quid of chewing tobacco in his wide jaws. "The Ranger tells me that ain't safe."

The dust cloud was nearer now, and the Apaches, aware their quarry had elected to stop, were fanning out. Tensleep spat. "This here's goin' to surprise 'em some. They reckon they're only comin' up on a hurt man an' a woman with kids."

It was cooler in the shade of the big rocks, and a glance at the *tinaja* showed a couple of barrels of water, at least. There was shelter for their horses and it was a good place to make a stand. Trust Tensleep to choose the right spot to fight a battle.

The desert before them was suddenly empty. The dust cloud had settled. The buzzard overhead had been joined by a hopeful relative. The buzzards were neutral. No matter who won down there, they would win. They had but to wait. The lizard had vanished. Bowdrie had dragged his saddle and bridle back into the rocks. He worked himself into a hollow in the sand, found a place for his elbows, and waited.

Nothing.

That was expected. It was when you never saw Apaches that you could worry. They were confident but did not wish to risk a death to get the four they pursued.

The woman was washing the man's arm now, replacing the bandage. Tensleep rolled his quid in his jaws and spat upon an itinerant scorpion. The scorpion backed off, unhappy at the unexpected deluge of trouble.

"How many would you say?"

Mooney thought it over. "Maybe ten. No less'n that. Could be twice as many."

"Tough."

"Yeah."

Mooney shoved his canteen at Bowdrie. "What are you? A camel? Don't you ever drink?"

"Forgot how." Bowdrie took a mouthful and let it soak the dry tissues, then swallowed.

Both men understood their chances of getting out alive were so slim they weren't worth counting on. The children stared at them, wide-eyed. The girl might have been ten, the boy two or three years younger. Their clothes were ragged but clean as could be expected after a hard ride. Bowdrie dug into his saddlebag and handed each child a piece of jerky. He grinned at them and winked. The girl smiled warily but the boy was fascinated by Bowdrie's guns. "Can I hold one?" he asked.

"I need 'em, son. Guns are dangerous things. You use 'em when need be, but nobody plays with a gun unless he's a fool." He indicated the area out in front of them. "This is one time they're needed."

Nothing moved out there; there was only sun, sand, and sky, low brush, occasional cactus, and the buzzards who seemed to simply hang in the sky, scarcely moving their wings. A shoulder showed, and Bowdrie held his fire.

Mooney glanced at him. "You're no tenderfoot."

"I grew up with 'em," Bowdrie commented. "Them an' Comanches."

That exposed shoulder had been an invitation, a test to see where they were, and how many. Yet they believed they knew. They had been chasing a man, a woman, and children.

A half-dozen Indians came off the ground at once. It was as if they were born suddenly from the sand. Where they appeared there had been nothing an instant before.

The thunder of suddenly firing rifles smashed echoes against the rocks and the whine of ricocheting bullets sent shuddering sounds through the clear desert air. An instant, a smell of gunpowder, and they were gone. Heat waves danced in the still air.

An Apache lay on his face not ten feet away. Another was sprawled near a clump of greasewood. As Bowdrie looked, that Indian rolled over and vanished before Bowdrie could bring his rifle to bear. There was blood on the sand where he had fallen.

"How'd you make out?"

"One down an' a possible," Bowdrie replied.

"Two down here, an' a possible. What's the matter? Can't you Rangers shoot no better than that?"

"You light a shuck," Bowdrie replied complacently. "I can outshoot you any day and twice on Sunday."

"Huh," Mooney grunted, then glanced at the scorpion, who was getting ready to move again. He spat, deluging it anew. Then suddenly he fired.

"Scratch another redskin," he said.

Bowdrie lay still, watching the desert. They were doing some thinking out there now. The two rifles had surprised them, and an Apache does not like to be surprised. Their attack had seemed so easy. The Apache is an efficient, able fighting man who rarely makes a useless move, and even more rarely miscalculates. This easy attack had now cost them three or four men and some wounds.

The sky was a white-hot bowl above them, the desert a reflector, yet the sun had already started its slide toward the far-off mountains.

An Apache moved suddenly, darting to the right. Bowdrie had his rifle on the spot where he had seen him drop from sight. He was a young warrior, and reckless. As he arose and moved, Bowdrie squeezed off his shot and the warrior stumbled.

Instantly, several more leaped up. Behind him a third rifle bellowed. So the father was back in action now. Bowdrie's second shot was a clean miss as the Indian dropped from sight.

"Got one!" The father spoke proudly. He crept closer

and Bowdrie wished he wouldn't. "Name is Westmore. Tried ranchin' down southwest of here. Mighty pretty country. They done burned us out whilst we was from home, so we run for it."

The shadows began to grow, the glare grew less. Bowdrie drank from the canteen. "I'd have had you tied to your saddle by now," he said.

Mooney chuckled. "Why, you track-smellin' soft-headed coyote! If these folks hadn't come along, you'd have been buzzard bait by now."

The woman looked surprised and curious. Westmore glanced from one to the other.

"Wished I could have got you without your guns," Bowdrie commented. "You're too good a man to shoot. I'd have been satisfied to take you in with my bare hands."

"You?" Mooney stared at him angrily. "Why, you long-horned maverick! I'd—!"

The Apaches tried it again, but this time it was cold turkey. Both men had spotted slight movements in the brush and were ready when they came up. Bowdrie got his before the Indian had his hands off the ground. Mooney fired at a rock behind where his Indian lay, dusting him with fragments.

"They'll wait until dark now," Mooney said. "I figure we've accounted for maybe half of them. We been shot with luck, you know that, don't you?"

"I know," Bowdrie agreed. "They just ran into more'n they were expecting but they'll have figured it out by now. No wounded man and a woman could be makin' the stand we are."

"Look!" Westmore pointed. Three Apaches were riding off into the distance. "They've quit."

Westmore started to rise but Bowdrie jerked him down. "It's an old trick," he explained. "Two or three ride off and the rest wait in ambush. When you start movin' around, they kill you."

The sun slid down behind the mountains in the distance and the desert grew cool. It was ever so. There was nothing to hold the heat, and night cooled things off very quickly. Stars came out and a coyote yipped, a coyote with a brown skin and a headband. Bowdrie dug into his saddlebag and brought out a piece of jerky for each. It was dry and tough but it lasted a long time and was nourishing. They chewed in silence.

A faint gray lingered, disappeared and gave birth to stars. Chick tossed his saddle blanket to the youngsters. Westmore peered from behind the rocks.

"You reckon those that left will come back with more?"

"Could be. In fact, it's more than likely."

"My name's Westmore," the man repeated, looking from one to the other.

"I'm Tensleep Mooney. This here's a Texas Ranger named Bowdrie. He's been on my trail for weeks."

The woman was puzzled. "He wants to arrest you? Why?"

"This gent here," Bowdrie said, "is too handy with a gun. The governor wants more taxpayers and this gent has been thinnin' down the population somethin' awful."

"But you'll let him go now, won't you?"

Mooney chuckled. "This here Sou-wegian ain't got me yet, an' it'll be a cold day in Kansas before he does."

"Soon as we're rid of these Apaches," Chick said, "I'll hog-tie you and take you back. I'll give you about two drinks between here an' Austin." He turned his head toward Westmore and his wife. "You know what this squatty good-for-nothin' did?

"He knows this country better than anybody. Knows ever' water hole. He passes one by, then swings back in the dark, gets him a drink, an' fills his canteen. Then he goes back to where I last saw him, lets me see him again, an' takes off in the dark. I have to follow him or lose him, so I've spent my days drier than a year-old buffalo chip!"

Talk died and they lay listening. There was no sound. Bowdrie turned to Mooney. "I'm goin' out there. There's at least one Apache out there, prob'ly more. I need a horse. When I get me a horse we'll light out. 'Paches don't like night fightin' an' we should make a run for it."

He dropped his gunbelts, then thrust one pistol into his waistband along with his bowie knife. He removed his spurs and jacket, then disappeared into the night.

The woman looked at Mooney. "Will he get back? How can he do this?"

"If anybody can do it," Mooney said, "he can. He's more Injun than many Injuns. Anyway, he's got no choice. He surely ain't goin' out of here a-foot."

There was a shallow arroyo nearby and Bowdrie found it and went down the sand bank to its bottom, then paused to listen.

He started on, paused again, hearing a faint sound he could not place, then went on. He was circling cautiously, feeling his way, when he heard a horse blow. He circled even wider, then dropped to the sand and crept nearer. He found them unexpectedly, six horses picketed in the bottom of the arroyo. Six horses did not necessarily mean six Indians, for some of the riders might already lie among the dead.

Try as he could, he saw no sleeping place, nor did he see any Indians or evidence of a fire, which they probably would not have, anyway.

Just as he was about to move toward the horses, an Indian arose from the ground and went to them. He moved around them, then returned to his bed on the sand a few yards away. When the Indian was quiet, Bowdrie moved to the horses. Selecting the nearest for his own, he drew the picket pins of all the horses, reflecting they must be stolen horses, for it was unlike Apaches to use picket pins, preferring the nearest bush or tree.

He moved to the horse he had chosen and swung to its back. The horse snorted at the unfamiliar smell and instantly there was movement from the Indian.

Slapping his heels to the horse, Bowdrie charged into the night, leading the other horses behind him. He turned at the flash of a gun and fired three quick shots into the flash.

Circling swiftly, he arrived at camp. "Roll out an' mount up!" he said. "We're leavin' out of here!"

He saddled swiftly, and they rode into the night. Three days later they rode into the dusty streets of El Paso. The Westmores turned toward New Mexico and the ranch of a relative. They parted company in the street and Mooney started for his horse. "Far enough, Mooney! Don't forget, you're my prisoner!"

"Your *what*?"

Mooney threw himself sidewise into an arroyo but Bowdrie did not move. "Won't do you a bit of good. Might as well give up! I've got you!"

"You got nothin'!" Mooney yelled. "Just stick your head around that corner and I'll—!"

"Be mighty dry where you're goin', Mooney. And you without a canteen."

"What? Why, you dirty sidewinder! You stole my canteen!"

"Borrowed it. You killed 'em all in fair fights, Mooney, so's you might as well stand trial. I'll ride herd on you so's you'll be safe whilst the trial's on.

"I've got the water, Mooney, and I have the grub, and the Baggs outfit has more friends here than you do. If you go askin' around, you'll really get your hide stretched. Looks to me like your only way is to come along with me."

There was silence and then Bowdrie said, "I will give you more than two drinks betwixt here an' Austin, Mooney. I was only makin' a joke about that."

There was no sound and Bowdrie knew what was happening. "If you're wise," he said loudly, "you'll come in an' surrender. No sense havin' an outlaw's name when you don't deserve it.

"I'll even testify for you. I'll tell 'em you were a miserable coyote not fit to herd sheep but that you're a first-class fightin' man."

Silence. Bowdrie smiled and walked back to his horse.

By now Mooney was headed out of town, headed back to the boondocks where he came from, but he'd come in, Bowdrie was sure of it. Just give him time to think it over.

He had warned him about El Paso, and he was too good a man to be in prison. Maybe a day would come when a Ranger couldn't use his own judgment, but Bowdrie had used his and was sure ninety percent of the others would agree. By now Tensleep was on his way to wherever he wanted to go.

Bowdrie walked his horse back down the street from the edge of town. This wasn't a bad horse, not as good as his roan waiting for him back in Laredo, but better than the bay lying dead in Sonora. The spare Indian horses he had given to Westmore. After all, they were going to start over with all too little.

Bowdrie tied his horse to the hitch-rail and went inside to the bar and ordered a cold beer. Taking it, he walked to a table and sat down.

Well, maybe he was wrong. Maybe McNelly wouldn't agree with his turning Mooney loose, but—

"All right, dammit!" Tensleep dropped into the chair opposite. "Take me in, if it makes you feel better. I just ain't up to another chase like that one." He looked at Bowdrie. "Can I keep my guns until I get there?"

"Why not?" Bowdrie looked around. "Bartender, bring the man a beer."

They sat without speaking, then Tensleep said, "You notice something? Those youngsters back there? Never a whimper out of 'em, an' they must have been scared."

"Sure they were scared. I was scared." Bowdrie glanced at Mooney, a reflective glint in his eye. "You know, Mooney, what you need is a wife. You need a home. Take some of that wildness out of you. Now, I—"

"You go to the devil," Mooney replied cheerfully.

HISTORICAL NOTE:

FORT GRIFFIN

This fort was established to restrain Comanche raids on settlers moving into the area, and a town catering to buffalo hunters sprang up around it. It was the nearest market south of Dodge City, and a supply point. Later, when the buffalo hunting had become a thing of the past, it became a stopping place on the Western Trail.

A wild, rough town with more than its quota of saloons, gambling houses, and other places of entertainment, it was a notorious hangout for some of the roughest and wildest of western characters as well as a stopping place for a good many sober, serious pioneers moving into the western country to build homes.

Pat Garrett, Billy the Kid, Bat Masterson, John W. Poe, Dave Rudabaugh, Jesse Evans, Jim East, Cape Willingham, and dozens of others paused in passing, some of them several times. It was here, according to the stories, that Wyatt Earp first met Doc Holliday.

The Road to Casa Piedras

Chick Bowdrie hooked his thumbs in his belt and watched the dancers. Old Bob McClellan and his two strapping sons were sawing away on their fiddles, lubricated by Pa Gardner's own make of corn whiskey.

Pa, flushed with whiskey and exertion, was calling the dances from a precarious platform of planks laid over three benches. Any platform would have been precarious, for Pa had been imbibing freely from his own keg of corn. Being the owner of the whiskey as well as the tin cup hanging from the spigot, he was the only one aside from the musicians who could take a drink without paying.

Emmy Chambers, blond and beautiful, whirled by Chick and smiled at him. A strand of her cornsilk hair had fallen over her eyes but she looked excited and happy. Chick couldn't see it himself, but womenfolks seemed to think a lot of dancing. Personally, he thought, it was better out on the sagebrush country with a good horse under him.

He never had been given to duding up, but lately some of the Rangers had been getting themselves some pretty slick outfits, so he followed the trend and had gotten himself up for this dance. He was wearing a black broadcloth shirt of the shield variety with a row of pearl buttons down each side, and for the first time in months he had his collar buttoned and was wearing a white string tie. It made his neck itch and he felt like he was tied with a rope halter.

His gunbelts were of black leather inlaid with mother-of-pearl and silver, likewise the holsters. His trousers were black, and he wore new hand-worked boots with California-style spurs with two-inch rowels, all shined up and pretty.

Emmy Chambers was the prettiest blond in the room, and Mary Boling the prettiest brunette. Mary was a dark-eyed girl with a hint of Spanish blood. This town was not his usual stamping grounds so he knew none of these people beyond a few names. He was about to leave when Emmy Chambers ran up to him.

"Chick, it isn't fair! Why aren't you out there dancing? Now, come on!"

"Now, ma'am," he protested, flushing, "I'm not a dancing man. I—" His words were cut off by the sharp report of a pistol shot, then another. An instant later they heard the pounding hooves of a racing horse.

Bowdrie caught up his hat and as he swung toward the door his eyes caught Mary Boling's. There was a strange brightness in them, almost a sort of triumph. Did that big cowhand affect her that way?

Chick stepped into the street, men and women crowding past him and around him.

Aside from the schoolhouse, where the dance was taking place, there was but one lighted window in the place, the stage station next door. With sudden realization, Bowdrie sprinted for the station. He was the first to arrive.

Shoving open the door, he saw John Irwin sprawled across his desk, his life's blood staining the clustered papers on which he had been working. His right hand dangled limply over the edge of the desk and his six-shooter lay on the floor beneath the hand. Irwin had died trying.

Bowdrie picked up the gun and sniffed the barrel. Then he checked the cylinder. The gun had been fired and one chamber was empty except for the cartridge shell.

"They got the money!" Ed Gardner exclaimed. "Twelve thousand dollars!"

Bowdrie glanced at him. "How'd you know that?" The fact that Irwin had the money in his safe was supposed to be known to but three men.

"When I stopped by before the dance, Irwin was countin' it."

Aside from Bowdrie himself, only Irwin, Sheriff Sam Butler, and Deputy Tom Robley were supposed to know the money was here. Butler and Robley had been at the dance. Bowdrie had seen them not three minutes before the shots were fired.

Bowdrie looked over at Butler. "You notify his folks, will you? No use doin' anything until morning. We'd just mess up whatever sign was left."

The crowd filed out and disappeared toward their homes. The dancing was over for tonight.

John Irwin had a cash deal for a herd of cattle, and as there had been several recent holdups, he notified the law that he would have the money on hand. Pa Gardner, who had seen the money, was not, despite his faults, a talkative man, yet somebody had known.

Bowdrie walked back to the schoolroom where the dance had taken place. A few couples stood around, reluctant to end the festivities or talking about the murder and robbery. Tom Robley was there.

"A pity," he said. "Irwin was a nice old man."

"Somebody else knew the money was there. If you come up with any names, let me know."

Tom stared at the knuckles of his big fists. He seemed unnaturally tense. "I will," he said, "believe me I will."

Mary Boling came over to them. "Hello, Tom!" Then to Chick, "You're the Texas Ranger, aren't you? I heard there was one in town."

Bowdrie's dark features were impassive. "You look mighty pretty in that dress," he commented.

She wrinkled her nose disdainfully. "This ol' thing?

It's all right, but I'll have prettier dresses. I'll be going to New Orleans for my clothes. Or to New York."

"You'll keep some young rancher busted," Bowdrie said dryly. "Clothes are costly."

"Maybe the man I marry won't be just a rancher." Mary tossed her curls, smiling at both of them. Tom Robley looked miserable.

"Ranchin' ain't so bad," Robley protested. "Anyway, Al Harshman's a rancher, and Jim Moody's a cowhand."

She laughed at him, squeezing his arm. "And you're a deputy sheriff!" she said. "But you might become almost anything. As for Al, he won't always be a rancher. Al's got ambition."

"So've I," Robley protested. "You'll see."

Ten miles out of town, Chick Bowdrie reined in the hammerhead roan, indicating the track on the edge of the shallow hole where rain had formed a pool.

"Headin' northeast. That track was made followin' the heaviest part of the rain, but before the last shower. Reckon he's our man, all right.

"Doesn't know the country too well. He's ridin' by landmarks. The trail's just a half-mile off to the east, but this gent is headed for Pistol Rock Spring, usin' that thumb butte over there for a marker."

"How d'you figure that?" Robley asked. He had believed he was a good man on a trail, yet he had seen very little since leaving town, while Bowdrie had ridden right along, only occasionally pointing out something he had seen.

"Twice he's swung too far west, and he's swung back until he's lined up on that butte. He's travelin' fast, so if he knew about that trail, he'd be usin' it. He wouldn't be afraid of meetin' anybody in this rain. Far as that goes, the trail isn't used much, anyway."

The three men rode on. Sam Butler had seen more than Robley, but not as much as Bowdrie. Tom's eyes were hollow from lack of sleep.

"He's got some help somewhere ahead," Bowdrie

commented, "or else he's a damn fool. No man in his right mind would run a horse like he has his unless he knew there was another waitin' for him. He's headin' right into that wasteland of the Horse Thief Mesa country."

The sun lifted over the brow of the hill and threw lances of sunlight across the sagebrush levels. Ahead lay the waste of Tobosa Flat, a flat stretch of creosote bush, tobosa, and burro grass. Here even the showers of the previous night had not settled the dust.

It was very hot. Their passing raised a dust cloud. If the man they pursued was watching his back trail, he knew he was followed. Then Bowdrie spotted the bush and rode over to it.

"Tied his horse here. Prob'ly either a stolen horse or one he just got hold of. It doesn't like him and he doesn't trust it. He tied fast instead of ground-hitching, an' when he started to get back into the saddle, it acted up. But let's see what he did when he got down from the saddle."

They trailed boot tracks to a nest of boulders on a low hill. There the man had knelt in the damp sand while watching his back trail. Had he seen them? They had not reached the dusty part at that time.

"Maybe daybreak, or right after. The first time he could see good, he stopped to look back." Bowdrie indicated a mark in the sand near where he had knelt. "Carries a rifle. Judging by the print of the butt plate, it could be a Winchester or a Henry, but that's just guessing."

He indicated the length of the man's stride. "Six feet tall, I'd say, weighs about one-seventy. Got a run-down heel on his right boot, and pretty badly run down. By the look of his tracks, I'd say he had something wrong with that leg. Else he's got an odd way of walkin'."

He went back to the bush where their own horses waited. He picked a black hair from the mesquite bush. "Black mane an' tail. From the stride I'd say about fourteen hands high. We'll have a picture of him real soon."

Butler agreed. Then he added, "You're like an Injun on a trail. Part of that trail back there I couldn't even see, yet you kept right on a-goin'."

"Instinct, maybe," Bowdrie said. "You pick up little things. Man on the run will usually keep to low ground until he wants to look back."

The desert became wilder and more barren. The mesquite thinned out and there was more burro grass. Even that became less and then they dipped down into a sandy draw littered with boulders. The man they followed had slowed to a walk here and Bowdrie did likewise. Pausing, he held up a hand for silence.

Nothing.

They rode up the slight incline and then the roan stopped suddenly, nervously.

Across the small, still pool of Pistol Rock Spring stood a bay horse; however, Bowdrie was not looking at the horse but at the sprawled body of a man. He had been shot three times through the stomach by somebody who could use a six-gun. The three holes in his chest might have been covered by a silver dollar.

The coffeepot lay on its side, most of the contents spilled into the sand. The dead man's gun was in its holster, and not far from the tethered bay was a saddle, but no rifle or scabbard.

"The man we followed must have killed this man for his horse," Butler suggested.

"No," Bowdrie said, "this is the man who killed Irwin. His partner waited here, shot him, and rode off with the loot.

"Look. See that run-down heel? An' the height and weight are about right. The other gent sat right over yonder. He let this man pick up the coffeepot in his right hand and then he shot him."

Bowdrie walked around the fire and the pool. There were the prints of boots, pointed toward the pool. The man had squatted here, his back against the rock, and from there he had killed the newcomer.

He glanced around. Tom Robley was staring at the dead man; he looked pale and shocked. "That's Jim Moody!" he said.

Butler came over and looked at the dead man's face. "That's Jim, all right. He was always a pretty good hand. Shot dead, an' he never had a chance."

Butler looked up. "Why, I wonder? Why would his own partner kill him?"

"Money. Moody held up Irwin an' killed him, but for all this second man knew, Moody was seen. But he didn't care. Moody pulled off the holdup, now this second man has all the loot. He's got twelve thousand dollars and he's scot-free."

"And we don't know anything about him," Butler said.

"We know a couple of things. He's a dead shot with a pistol, and he's left-handed. Also, he was somebody who knew Jim Moody."

"Left-handed?" Robley asked.

"He sat with his back braced against that rock, waitin'. He smoked cigarettes. Now, you just take a look at those two stubs of cigarettes and the burned matches. They are on the left side of the fire. If he was right-handed, they would be on the right side.

"He waited, smokin', and he flipped the cigarette stubs an' matches into the fire. Some didn't make it.

"Somethin' here I don't understand. The killer took Moody's saddle. He was ridin' a bronc saddle with an undercut fork. That saddle was dropped right over yonder an' you can see where the fork butted into the wet sand. He also took the rifle Moody had."

"It figures," Butler agreed. "So far as I know, Moody never rode over this way. He rode for the Circle W away the other side of town. He never rode in except to see his girl. I doubt if he knew anything about this part of the country."

"Somethin' else that's curious. That mark to the right

side of his right boot. That mark was made by a holster touching the sand. Now, if this gent is left-handed, why does he wear his gun on the right side?

"Unless . . . unless he wears it for a cross-draw? If he wore that gun in front of his right hip an' had his right side toward a man, he could draw almighty fast."

Tom Robley's head came up sharply, his eyes filled with a dawning realization. Bowdrie stared at him. "Tom, d'you know anybody like that?"

Robley flushed. "I ain't sure," he muttered. "I just ain't sure."

Bowdrie looked down at the dead man, but in his mind he was studying the young deputy. Robley had been acting very strange. His reaction to this situation was odd, and had been so from the beginning. Since they had found Jim Moody's body he had seemed upset, almost frightened.

What could Tom Robley know? Did he have a clue they did not possess? Always, in any criminal situation, human passions and feelings are involved, and Bowdrie knew too little of the townspeople and their relationships with each other.

Bowdrie mounted and began casting for a trail. He knew he had his work cut out for him. The killer did not intend to be followed and was using every trick in the book. He had brushed out the tracks where his horse had stood waiting, so there were no identifying tracks. Nearby there was a wide, rocky shelf several acres in extent where he would leave no tracks. Searching for the place where he left the rock shelf, Bowdrie found nothing.

After two hours of fruitless searching Bowdrie sat his saddle looking out over a waste of scattered tar bush, yeso, and tobosa. There was no trail.

Tom Robley suddenly broke the silence. "I'm headin' for town. Nothin' more to be done here." Without waiting for a reply, he turned back toward town.

Butler stared after him. "Now, what's eatin' that youngster? Never seen him cut up so."

Bowdrie was concerned with the matter at hand. Moody was dead and Robley would report it in town. But what did he know about the man they must now pursue? That he was utterly ruthless, left-handed, and knew this desert well. The rock shelf was no accident. The man had planned well. That was indicated by his choice of a meeting place. Bowdrie gestured toward Moody's body. "He was a tool, Butler. The real criminal is the man who killed him. He worked all this out ahead of time."

Bowdrie was searching for more than an obvious trail across the desert. He was trying to find the trail left by the man's secret thoughts. Each move the man made helped to outline his character. His cold-blooded planning indicated he did not intend to leave the country. If he had so planned, he would have paid less attention to his trail and just kept going.

He had been looking, looking . . . His eyes caught at something tangled in the cat claw. It was a low clump of the brush growing close to the ground. One of its vicious thorns had caught . . .

Burlap!

He held up the thin strand to Butler. "Wrapped his horse's hooves in burlap sacking so's it would leave no trail. No wonder we couldn't find where he left the rock shelf."

He swung to the saddle. "Sam, that gent, whoever he is, won't be wanderin' around. He won't travel fast with that sackin' on his horse's hooves. From here there's just three trails that lead to water. To Horse Thief Mesa, to Casa Piedras, or to someplace on the upper Cibolo."

"My guess would be either of the first two. He wouldn't be gettin' noplace goin' up to Cibolo."

Bowdrie agreed. "You take the Casa Piedras trail. I'll head for the mesa. Scout for some of that burlap fiber, or tracks. If you see any, holler or give a shot."

They separated and Bowdrie began painstakingly to search the desert, yet scarcely ten minutes had gone by when he heard a long cowboy yell from Butler. When he rode over to him Butler pointed out a thin thread of burlap caught on some prickly pear.

For an hour they followed at a walk, picking up occasional smudges or signs of passage. Suddenly the trail they followed merged with a cattle trail and the ground was torn by their passing.

Butler swore. "Lost him! Too many critters come this way."

"We'll follow along. He'll get rid of that burlap soon, I think."

A mile farther they found it, half-buried in hurriedly kicked-up sand. Bowdrie picked it from the sand, shook it out, and brought it along. From time to time as they rode he turned it over as if trying to read something from the sacking itself. Then he stowed it in one of his half-empty saddlebags.

In Casa Piedras Bowdrie called to a Mexican boy. "Want to feed and water these horses? Then bring them back and tie them here." He tossed the boy a bright silver dollar.

Bowdrie glanced at a horse hitched nearby as Butler joined him on the walk. "That steeldust's wearing a bronc saddle with an undercut fork," he commented, "and the horse has been ridden hard."

"Let's eat," Butler suggested. "I'm hungry as a Panhandle wolf!"

It was boardinghouse style, and Bowdrie seated himself, turning a cup right-side-up, then reaching for the coffee. Another hand reached at the same time and only Chick's dexterity prevented the pot from being upset. Bowdrie looked around into a pair of frosty blue eyes. The man had reached for the pot with his left hand. Chick smiled.

"Help yourself!" he suggested. "Coffeepots are bad luck when they are upset."

Sam Butler nodded sagely. He speared a triple thickness of hotcakes and lifted them to his plate. "Sure is. Wust kind of bad luck."

The frosty eyes turned ugly. For an instant they flickered to the badge on Butler's chest, then shifted to Bowdrie.

"Uh-huh," Bowdrie agreed. "I knew a gent once who got drilled right through the heart whilst holding a coffeepot in his right hand. Never had a chance."

"Sho nuff?" A big blond cowhand at the end of the table glanced up. "A man surely couldn't let go of a pot fast enough, could he?"

"That's what the murderer figured," Bowdrie replied. "This just happened a few hours ago, over at Pistol Rock Springs."

The cowhand stared but the man with the frosty blue eyes continued to eat. "Been to those springs many a time," the cowhand said. "Who was it got hisself killed?"

"Name of Jim Moody. He robbed the stage station over yonder last night, shot John Irwin, then cut across country to the spring. His partner was waitin', an' the way he was ridin', I figure Moody expected his partner had a fresh horse waitin'. Instead of that he got lead for breakfast. This partner of his shot him, took the money, and lit out."

"Now, that's a dirty skunk if I ever heard of one!" the blond cowhand said. "He ought to be hung! Hell, I knew Jim Moody! He used to spark that Boling gal from over the way. Seen him at dances, many's the time." He turned to the man with the frosty blue eyes. "Sho, Al! I reckon you won't be none put out. I've heard tell there was a time you was sweet on that Boling gal yourself!"

Al shrugged. "Talked to her a few times, that's all. Same as you did."

Something clicked in Bowdrie's brain. Al . . . Al Harshman, a rancher. The ambitious one.

Al got to his feet. "I'll be ridin'," he said, to nobody in particular. Then he asked, "How much did he get away with?"

"Twelve thousand," Bowdrie replied, his face inscrutable. Al was wearing his gun on the right side, butt forward, and pulled slightly to the front. "But he won't have it long, Harshman. He left a plain trail."

Harshman stiffened angrily and seemed about to reply, then turned toward the door. He glanced back. "I wouldn't want the job of trailin' him," he commented. "He might prove right salty if cornered."

"When a man is murdered without a chance," Bowdrie commented, "we Rangers make it a point of honor to hunt him down. A Ranger will get that killer if it is the last thing he ever does."

"Rangers can die."

"Of course, but we never die alone." Bowdrie smiled. "We always like to take somebody with us."

When he had gone outside, Butler glanced over at Bowdrie. "How'd you know his name was Harshman?"

"He looked like a harsh man," Bowdrie replied, smiling.

Strolling to the porch outside, Bowdrie sat down on the bench after retrieving the burlap sacking from the saddlebag. He began to go over it with painstaking care. The Mexican boy who had returned the horses stood watching, eyes bright with curiosity. "What you look for, *señor?*"

"Somethin' to tell me who the hombre was who used this sack. Nobody uses anything for long without leaving his mark on it."

The outside of the sacking was thick with damp sand; much more must have come off in his saddlebags, Bowdrie reflected unhappily. Stretching the fibers, he searched them with keen eyes. Suddenly the Mexican boy reached over and plucked a gray hair from the sacking, then another.

"So? He had a gray or steeldust horse, Pedro?"

"The name is Miguel, *señor,*" the boy protested, very seriously. He bent over the sack, pointing at a fragment of blue clay. "See? It is blue. The sack has lain near a well."

"Near a well, Pedro? Why do you say that?"

"The name is Miguel, *señor*. Because there is the blue clay. Always in this country there is blue clay in the hole of wells, *señor*. Always, it is so."

"Thanks, Pedro. You'd make a good Texas Ranger."

"I? A Texas Ranger? You think so, *señor*?" His expression changed. "But, *señor*, the name is not Pedro. It is Miguel. Miguel Fernández."

"All right, Pedro." Bowdrie stood up. "Just as you say."

He glanced once more at the sacking, and suddenly, in the crease near the seam, he noticed a tiny fragment of crushed, somewhat oily pulp. He took it out, studied it, then folded it into a cigarette paper.

"Wait for me," he said to Butler.

Swiftly he crossed the street to the store. A little old man with gold-rimmed spectacles looked up. Bowdrie asked him a question, then another. The old man replied, studying him curiously.

Bowdrie walked back to Butler. "Let's go. I think we've got our man. I only hope we'll be in time."

"In time?" Butler asked. "In time for what?"

The Mexican boy caught his hand. "*Señor!*" he pleaded. "If I am to be a Ranger, you must know my name! It is Miguel! Miguel Fernández!"

Bowdrie chuckled and handed him another dollar. "If you say so, Pedro! Miguel it is! *Adiós*, Pedro!"

He swung to the saddle and started out of town, Butler beside him. "In time for what?" he repeated.

"To prevent another killing," Bowdrie told him.

"Robley knew," Bowdrie continued. "He guessed it when he saw the dead man was Jim Moody. He knew who it was when I said the killer was left-handed. He was away ahead of us."

"You think it was Harshman? But how could he have known about the money? For that matter, how did Moody find out?"

The desert flat gave way to rising ground, the hillsides scattered with juniper. The sage had taken on a deeper color and there were clumps of grama grass.

Chick dipped into an arroyo and skirted a towering wall of red sandstone, into a shaded canyon, then across another flat. The trail dipped again and they rode into the yard of a lonely ranch house. Nearby there were several pole corrals and three saddled horses.

Bowdrie dropped to the ground. As his feet touched the earth, Al Harshman stepped from the door. Narrow-eyed, faint perspiration showing on his brow, he looked from Butler to Bowdrie and back. "Huntin' somethin'?"

"You," Bowdrie said. "I am arrestin' you for the murder of Jim Moody and complicity in the robbery and murder of John Irwin."

Harshman took a step into the yard. He was smiling, a taunting smile.

"All you've got is suspicion. You can't prove nothin'. I ain't been away from here but that ride to town, where you saw me."

He smiled again. "You can't prove I was anywhere near Pistol Rock Spring. And how would I know about the money? How would Moody know?"

"I know how you knew about the money." Tom Robley stepped around the corner of the house. His eyes flickered to Bowdrie and back. "I'd have beat you here, but I was looking for the girl first."

"What girl?" Butler demanded.

"Mary Boling. It was she told them about the money. She with all her talk about New Orleans and fancy clothes. She put poor Jim Moody up to it. She's partly responsible for both Irwin an' Moody bein' dead. Me, I'm mostly responsible."

"You?" Butler exclaimed. "Now, Tom, you just—"

"Don't get me wrong. I'd nothin' to do with stealin' the money or the killing. It was my mouth. I was so busy tryin' to convince Mary what an important job I had that I just ran off at the mouth. Because of my loose tongue, two good men are dead."

Harshman laughed. "You think Mary had a hand in it? You're a fool, Tom Robley, a double-damned fool.

Suppose you had told Mary? What could that mean to me?"

Chick Bowdrie stood listening and curious. Watching the scene, every sense alert, quick to hear every word, he was also aware that three saddled horses, packed for the trail, stood at the corral.

The big rancher wore a dark blue shirt, two of the front buttons unfastened. His boots were highly polished, and he looked quite the dandy. Bowdrie smiled, understanding a few things.

"You're pretty sure of yourself, Al, but Sam Butler and me, we trailed you. We know a left-handed man sat against a rock at Pistol Rock Spring and smoked cigarettes. He tossed the matches at the fire with his left hand.

"We trailed you from the spring, and it wasn't even hard. You wrapped your horse's hooves in burlap sacking so you wouldn't leave a trail. We have the sacks."

Harshman shrugged. "There are a lot of sacks around. Can you prove those sacks were mine? Don't be foolish! Those sacks could have belonged to anybody."

"I found gray horsehairs that will match your gelding, and there's blue clay on them, as there is around your well."

"So? There's blue clay around half the wells in the county, and as for horsehairs, how many gray horses are there?"

"We've got somethin' else, Al," Bowdrie said. "Folks told me you were ambitious. That you had brains. Mary spoke mighty highly of you back there at the dance.

"You were smart, all right. You had ideas. You decided to try something new, Al. You had some cottonseed shipped in here so you could try planting it."

"So? Is that criminal?"

"Not at all. You were away ahead of everybody else around this part of the country. You sent for cottonseed and you got it. Some of it came in that sack you used, Al. I found some of the cottonseed in the sack."

"*Bowdrie!*" Robley shouted. "*Look out!*" Robley's hand

slashed down for a gun, and a shotgun roared from the
window of the house and Tom Robley staggered, firing
toward the house.

It was one of those breathtaking instants that explode
suddenly, and Bowdrie saw Harshman grab for a gun—
with his *right* hand!

The hand darted into the gaping shirtfront and the
gun blasted, but a split second late. Bowdrie had palmed
his six-gun and fired, then took a long step forward and
right, firing again as his foot came down.

Al Harshman was on his knees, his face contorted
with shock and hatred. Vaguely Bowdrie knew other
guns were firing, but this was the man he had to get.
Harshman had dropped the derringer hideout gun and
was coming up with his other pistol.

Bowdrie held his fire and the gun slipped from
Harshman's fingers.

Butler was at the cabin door, gun in hand. Robley
was down, covered with blood.

Sam Butler turned to Bowdrie, his face gray. "I never
killed no woman before," he muttered. "Dammit,
Bowdrie, I—!"

"You did what you had to do. Anyway," he added
practically, "it might have been Tom."

Robley was dying. Bowdrie knew it when he knelt
beside him. "Mary? Wha . . . happened?"

"Mary's gone, Tom. She was killed. So is another
man in there."

"Her brother," Butler said. "We didn't even know he
was around."

"Mary . . . it was Al all the time," Robley was saying.
"It wasn't Jim or me."

He lay quiet and Bowdrie got slowly to his feet. "Too
bad," he said. "He was a good man."

"All because she was greedy. She couldn't be content
with the looks she was born with an' clothes like the
other gals had." Butler swore softly, bitterly.

"Me," Bowdrie said, "all I want is a good horse under

me, the creak of a saddle, and a wind off the prairies in
my face.

"An' maybe, Sam, just like you, maybe I want to
make things a little more peaceful for other folks. A
man can't build anything or even make a living when
there's somebody ready to take it from him."

"Maybe that's it," Butler said. "Maybe you just said
it. I never could figure why I took this job in the first
place."

Butler walked to his horse, and Bowdrie followed.
"Ain't more than six miles over to the Fernández place.
She fixes the best *frijoles* anyplace around. We'll just
ride over there an' hire him to haul these bodies into
town."

"All right," Bowdrie said, "let's ride over an' see
Pedro."

"Miguel," Sam Butler said. "The name is Miguel!"

HISTORICAL NOTE:

JOHN RINGO

This is a short version of what was said to be his proper name, Ringgold. A mysterious character, evidently of some education, he was born in Missouri in 1844. He took part in the Mason County War as a follower of Scott Cooley, and was arrested. He broke jail and escaped to Arizona. There he allied himself with Old Man Clanton and his boys, and with Curly Bill Brocius.

He killed a harmless man named Louis Hancock for ordering beer when Ringo wanted him to drink whiskey, and he participated in the ambush of a mule train packing silver in Skeleton Canyon.

Just why Ringo was considered so dangerous doesn't show in his record. Perhaps it was because he was mean and surly when drinking and of uncertain temper at any time. A sort of legend has grown up about his name, perhaps because it has a nice sound, and it has been used in many stories, including the movie Stage-coach. I have read a thousand lines telling of how dangerous he was without one line of evidence to prove it.

A Ranger Rides to Town

Morning lay sprawled in sleepy comfort in the sunlit streets. The banker's rooster, having several times proclaimed the fact that he was up and doing, walked proudly toward the dusty street. The banker, his shirttail hanging out, was just leaving the front door accompanied by two men, both dusty from hard riding.

Outside the bank a rider clad in a linen duster sat astride a blood bay with his rifle across his knees and the reins of three other horses in his hands. The fourth man of the group leaned against a storefront some twenty yards away with a rifle in his hands.

The bank's door was already wide open and the banker and his escort disappeared within.

East of town the dry wash had been bridged and the sound of a horse's hooves on that bridge was always audible within the town. Now, suddenly, that bridge thundered with the hoofbeats of a hard-ridden horse, and the two men in the street looked sharply around.

Behind his house, Tommy Ryan, thirteen years old and small for his age, was splitting wood. He glanced around in time to see a man on a hammerhead roan, the horse's sides streaked with sweat, charge into the street. The man wore a black flat-crowned hat and the two guns in his hands were not there for fun.

The man in the linen duster was closest, and he hesitated, waiting to see who or what was approaching. When he saw a rider with pistols in his hand and a Ranger's badge on his chest, he lifted his rifle, but too late. The rider's bullet cut a long furrow the length of his forearm and smashed his elbow. The rifle fell into the dust. Numb with shock, the rider sat gripping his arm and staring.

The rifleman down the street caught the second bullet just as he himself fired. He stood for an instant, then turned and walked three steps and fell on his face. One spur rowel kept turning a moment after he fell.

When the shooting was over, one of the banker's escorts lay sprawled in the doorway, gun in hand, and the Ranger stood over him, gun in hand, staring into the shadowy precincts of the bank.

Another man with a badge pushed his way through the crowd that gathered. "Hi, Bowdrie! I'm Hadley, sheriff. I didn't know there were any Rangers in the country."

"Looks like I got here just in time," Bowdrie commented. He kept a pistol in his hand.

"Some shootin'," a bystander commented.

"Surprise," Bowdrie said. "They didn't expect anybody to come shooting. I had an edge."

Sheriff Hadley led the way into the bank. Two men lay dead on the floor, one of them the banker. He had been shot through the head at close range.

"He was a good man," Hadley said. "The town needed him." He glanced around. "You scored a clean sweep. You got 'em all."

"That's what it looks like," he agreed. His eyes swept the scene with a swift, all-seeing glance. Then he went past the bodies and into the private office of the banker. It was cool there, and undisturbed.

Bowdrie paused for a long minute, looking around, considering not only what he saw but what he had just seen. This room had been the seat of a man's pride, of his life's work. He had been a man who was building something, not only for himself and those who followed, but for his country. This man was putting down roots, enabling others to do the same.

Now he was dead, and for what? That some loose-gunned wastrels might have a few dollars to spend on whiskey and women.

He turned to look back into the bank, where Hadley was squatting beside the bodies. "No business today, Hadley. I want the bank closed."

"Young Jim Cane can handle it," Hadley said. "He's a good man."

"Nevertheless, I want the bank closed for business. I want to look around. Don't explain, just close it."

Tommy Ryan stared wide-eyed at the Ranger. He had been hearing stories of Chick Bowdrie but had never seen a real live Ranger before. Bowdrie's eyes wandered the street, studying the storefronts, the upstairs windows. Who might have been a witness? In a town of early risers, somebody must have seen what happened before the holdup.

"Anything I can do?" The man was tall and well-set-up, with blond hair and friendly eyes. "I'm Kent Friede. I was a friend of Hayes's."

"Nothin' anybody can do, Kent. Hayes never had a chance. Shot right through the skull. Bowdrie here come in on 'em and made a cleanup. He got 'em all."

"No," Bowdrie said quietly, oblivious of the startled glances from Hadley and Friede. "I got three. But I didn't shoot at that man inside the bank and he didn't shoot Hayes."

"What?" Hadley turned on him. "Then who—?"

"There was a fifth man who never appeared in the operation. He killed both Hayes and the outlaw inside the bank."

"I don't follow," Friede said. "How could that be?"

Bowdrie shrugged. "Who runs the bank now? Is it this Jim Cane you mentioned?"

"If there's anything left to run. Lucky they didn't get away with any money."

"It's my guess they did get the money," Bowdrie said. "The fifth man got it, and it's my bet he knew where to look."

"You're implying it was an inside job?" Friede was obviously skeptical. "I don't believe that. Jim Cane's a fine young man. We all trust him."

Bowdrie waved a hand. "Close it up, Hadley, and give me the key. Some things don't fit, but they will before I'm through."

Yet as he walked along the street he was far from feeling confident. The outlaw with the broken arm had been taken to jail and must be questioned. Bowdrie had an idea he would know nothing. The man who planned this job would have been shrewd enough to communicate with only one man, undoubtedly the outlaw killed inside the bank. At least, that was how it looked now.

He believed there was a fifth man involved, but it was no more than a theory and one that might not hold water.

First, his own arrival had not been by chance. He had been tipped that a robbery was planned. Who had tipped him, and why? Who had thrown that note wrapped around a rock into his campsite only a few hours ago? A note that warned him of the holdup and how it was to be carried out? At first glance he had seen that the banker had been killed from close up. Also, when he entered the bank there had been a thin blue tinge of tobacco smoke in the office air, and the smell of tobacco. None of the outlaws had been smoking, nor had the harried banker.

Nor was there any reason for them to enter the private office. The huge old safe was against the back wall some distance away, and it was before this safe that Hayes had been murdered. A man standing in the door of the private office could have fired that shot, yet all Bowdrie's man-hunting experience told him no outlaws would have been in that position. But suppose a man had already been hidden inside the bank?

A small boy stood nearby in bare feet and Bowdrie

glanced down into the wide blue eyes and the freckled face. "Hi, podner! Is this your town?"

"Yup! My pa sank the first well ever dug in this county!"

"Rates him high in my book," Bowdrie said. "Any man who brings water to a dry country deserves credit."

"You stayin' in town?"

"For a little while, I guess. I've got to find the men who did this." He paused. "It was a dirty deal, son, because there was another man in on this. He not only shot Banker Hayes in the back, he double-crossed his own pals."

The boy nodded seriously. By his own standards as well as those of the country in which he lived, the two crimes were among the worst of which a man could be accused.

All was quiet at the jail when he arrived. The wounded outlaw was lying on his bunk staring at the ceiling. Reluctantly he sat up when Bowdrie came to the bars. "You should have killed me," he said bitterly. "I ain't cut out for no prison. I'll die in there."

"Maybe you won't have to go," Bowdrie said.

"What's that?"

"If you can tell me who was in on this job, you might go free. Who was waiting inside the bank?"

"Huh?" The outlaw was obviously surprised. "Inside? Nobody. The boys went after Hayes. He opened the bank door." He paused, frowning. "Come to think on it, the banker just walked in. The door was already unlocked. But how could anybody be inside?"

"You tell me." Bowdrie studied the man. The outlaw was surprised and disturbed. "Who planned this job?"

"I dunno. They come to me an' asked if I'd like to go as horse-holder. I'd done a few things with one of those boys before, so I went along. We wasn't to use no names. Nobody was supposed to ask questions. Him who was killed inside, he was ridin' herd on us. He set this up if anybody did."

"Where was the split to be made?"

"Well"—the outlaw hesitated—"it was to be made after. After we got away, I mean. Nothin' much was said about it. We done taken it for granted, like."

"The man who was killed down by the store. Did you know him?"

"Seen him around. He was rounded up, just like me. Those boys had a job planned and they needed help. We wasn't any organized outfit, if that's what you mean."

"Was there any talk about money?"

"Sure! That's why we done it. The big feller, the one who was killed inside, he said we'd make five hundred apiece from it, maybe more. That there's a lot of money for somebody like me. Hell, I on'y worked seven months last year, at thirty dollars a month. Stole a few head of stock here'n there, never made more than drinkin' money."

Chick Bowdrie went back to his horse, and mounting, rode out of town. That he was being watched, he knew. Out of curiosity? Or fear? Suspicion was growing, centering around young Cane, who would inherit whatever the banker left.

Easy as that solution was, and Bowdrie could think of a half-dozen reasons for believing it, that simple answer left him uneasy and unconvinced. Riding out of town, he circled around until he could pick up the incoming trail of the four outlaws.

They could have reached town no more than fifteen minutes before he himself. That meant they must have been camped not too far from town, and might have been visited by whoever the inside man had been.

Slowly, a pattern was beginning to shape itself in Bowdrie's mind, although he was careful to remember it was no more than a possibility.

The inside man had known there was money in the bank and he had made contact with an outlaw, perhaps somebody he had known before. At his suggestion that outlaw had rounded up a few men to pull off the job. None of them were to know anything. If captured they would be unable to tell anything because they knew nothing.

It was early and nobody had come over the trail since the arrival of the outlaws. He picked up their trail without difficulty. They had made no effort to hide their tracks, until suddenly, by intent or accident, their trail merged with that of a herd of horses. He was more than two hours in working out their trail.

At first it held to dry washes and then wove through mesquite groves higher than the head of a man on horseback. Almost an hour of riding brought him to a campfire of ashes and a few partly burned sticks. He stirred the ashes and found no embers, but when he felt the ash with his fingers, there was still warmth.

Dividing the camp into quarters, he searched each section with meticulous care. They had eaten here, and they had drunk coffee. There had been four men who were joined by a fifth man who sat with them. This man had sat on the ground, one leg outstretched. His spur had gouged the sand and there were faint scratches near the upper part of the boot.

Studying the situation carefully, he then mounted and rode in careful circles, ever-widening, around the camp. He drew up suddenly. Here, behind a clump of mesquite, a man had crouched, spying on the outlaw camp. Bowdrie muttered irritably. The roan twitched an ear and Bowdrie glanced up. The horse was looking toward the trail with both ears pricked and his nostrils expanding. Speaking softly to the horse, Bowdrie waited, ready.

A rider pushed through the mesquite and came toward them at a fast trot, but his eyes were on the ground and did not see Bowdrie until he was quite near. He drew up sharply. It was Kent Friede.

"Find anything?" Was there an edge to his tone?

"Not much. They camped back yonder, an' they had a visitor."

"Ah!" Friede nodded. "I suspected as much! Most likely Cane rode out here to give them information."

"What makes you suspect Cane? Anybody might have done it."

"Who else would gain by Hayes's death?"

Bowdrie shrugged, sitting easy on his horse. Something about Friede bothered him, and he decided he would not want to turn his back on him. It was just a feeling, and probably a foolish one. It was never wise to jump to conclusions. What he wanted was evidence.

"I've not met Cane. What's he like?"

"About twenty-five. Nice-looking man. He's been a cowhand, and he drove a freight wagon. Lately he's been working in a store."

"How'd he come to be Hayes's heir?"

"Hayes cottoned to him from the first time they met, and now he's about to marry Hayes's daughter. He works part-time in the bank, with Hayes. After the bank closes, he goes over to the store."

Jim Cane was in the Caprock Saloon with Hadley when they walked in. He was a rangy young man with dark red hair and a hard jaw. He looked more like a rider than a banker. Cane turned as they entered and his eyes slanted quickly from one to the other. Bowdrie felt his pulse skip a beat as he saw Cane. A few years had changed him a lot.

"Find anything?" Hadley asked. The sheriff was a stalwart man, a leather-hard face and cool, careful eyes. A good man to have on your side, a bad man to have on your trail.

"Not much." Bowdrie explained about the campfire and the visitor. He did not mention the unseen watcher, nor what he had found near the campfire.

"All right to get back to business at the bank?" Cane asked. There was a shade of belligerence in his tone. "I've ranchers coming in for their payroll money."

"Will you have the money they need?"

"I've sent to Maravillas for it. We lost eight thousand dollars," he added.

"Payroll money? Somebody must have known it would be there."

"Everybody knew. We've been supplying ranchers with payroll money for years."

"Eight thousand? That could hurt to lose. Can you make out?"

"You mean, will it break the bank? No, it won't. That bank belongs to Mary Jane now, and I won't let it break." He spoke with cool determination, yet there was something more in his tone. A warning?

"You should make out," Friede commented, "as long as no rumors get started. What if there was a run on the bank?"

Jim Cane turned his eyes to Friede. "You'd like that, wouldn't you? You'd like to see Mary Jane broke and me thrown out."

Bowdrie watched the two men. Hadley had tightened up, ready to avert trouble if it began. Out of such a quarrel might come something revealing.

Friede put down his glass. "I've no trouble with either of you. If Hayes wanted to take in a saddle tramp, that was his business, and if Mary Jane wants to marry a drifter, that's hers."

Cane balled his fists. "Why, you—!"

"Easy does it!" Hadley interrupted. "Kent, you watch your tongue. I've seen men killed for no more than that."

Friede shrugged contemptuously. His face was white and drawn, but not with fear. This man when cornered could be deadly. "Don't start anything, Cane, or I'll have my say. Some people don't like wet stock."

Jim Cane looked as if he had been slapped, but before he could reply Kent Friede turned away, an ugly triumph in his expression. Cane stared after him and his hand shook as it lifted to the bar as if to steady himself. Then without a word he walked out.

Hadley stared after them. "Now, what did he mean by that?" Hadley glanced at Bowdrie. "Friede seems to know more than he lets on."

Bowdrie made no comment, but behind his dark, Indian-like features his mind was working swiftly. The deep, dimplelike scar beneath his cheekbone seemed deeper, and his face had grown colder. Leaving Hadley in the saloon, he crossed to the bank.

There were things here he must check before the bank was permitted to reopen, but more than that he wanted to be alone, to think. Letting himself in, he closed and locked the door behind him, then stood looking around.

It was late afternoon and the sun was going down. Most of the townspeople were at home preparing for supper. Only hours before, two men had died here, killed by a man they trusted, but who was the man?

For almost an hour he sat in the banker's chair reconstructing the crime by searching through his experience and what little he had learned for the motivation. After a while he went to the old filing cabinet and rummaged through the papers there and in the desk. Finally he stepped out on the street, locking the door behind him.

The Hayes house was just down the street and he turned that way. In answer to his knock the door was opened by a slender, dark-haired girl with lovely eyes. Eyes red from crying. "Oh? You must be the Ranger? Will you come in?"

Bowdrie removed his hat and followed her through the ornate old parlor with its stiff-collared portraits of ancestors to a spacious and comfortable living room. He realized then that he had come to the wrong door. The parlor entrance or "front door" was rarely used in these houses. The kitchen door was the usual entrance. The table, he noticed as he glanced into the dining room, was set for three, although but one plate was in use.

"Please don't let me interrupt your supper," he protested.

She glanced at him quickly, embarrassed. "I . . . I set Dad's place, too. Habit, I guess."

"Why not? And the other is for Jim Cane?"

"Have you seen him? I've been so worried. He's

taking this awfully hard. He . . . he loved Dad as much as I did."

Her voice was low and he caught the emotion in it and changed the subject.

"I hope to finish my work tomorrow and be riding on, but there are some things you could tell me. Was Kent Friede sweet on you? I mean, was he a suitor?" Bowdrie could not recall ever using the expression before, but believed it was the accepted one. There was so much he did not know about how people talked or conducted themselves. So much he wanted to know.

"Sort of. As much as he could be on anyone. Kent's mostly concerned with himself. Then . . . well, he's not the sort of man a girl would marry. I mean . . . he's killed men. He is very good with a gun. The best around here, unless it is Sheriff Hadley."

Bowdrie's black eyes met hers. His expression was mildly amused. "You wouldn't marry a gunfighter?"

She flushed. "Well, I didn't mean that . . . exactly."

Bowdrie smiled, and she was startled at how warm and pleasant it made him look. He had seemed somehow grim and formidable. Maybe it was because she knew who he was. "Your coffee's good." She had almost automatically filled his cup. "Even a gunfighter can enjoy it. But I know what you mean. You want to be sure when you cook supper there's somebody there to eat it."

The door opened suddenly and there was a jingle of spurs and Jim Cane stood framed in the opening. His face was drawn and worried. His eyes went sharply from Bowdrie to Mary Jane. "You here? Why can't you let this girl alone? She's lost her father, and—"

"Jim!" Mary Jane protested. "Mr. Bowdrie has been very nice. We have been talking and sharing some coffee. Why don't you sit down and we will all have supper?"

"Maybe the Ranger won't be able to. There's been a killing. Kent Friede was found dead just a few minutes ago."

Bowdrie put down his cup. He had been looking forward to a quiet supper. It was not often he ate with people. "Who found him?"

"I did." Cane stared defiantly. "He was lying in the alley behind the bank, and if you think I killed him, you're dead wrong!"

"I didn't say . . ." Bowdrie got to his feet. "Thank you, Miss Hayes."

Kent Friede lay on his face in the alley back of the bank with a knife between his shoulder blades, a knife driven home by a sure, powerful hand. His body was still warm.

A half-dozen men stood around as Bowdrie made his examination. Chick was thinking fast as he got to his feet.

This was all wrong. Kent Friede was not the man to let another get behind him. Nor was there any cover close by. The alley was gravel and not an easy place to creep up on a man unheard. This was cold-blooded murder, but one thing he knew. It had not happened in this alley.

He withdrew the knife and studied it in the light of a lantern. He held it up. "Anybody recognize this?"

"It's mine!" Tommy Ryan's eyes were enormous with excitement. "It's my knife! I was throwin' it this afternoon. Throwin' it at a mark on that ol' corner tree!"

Bowdrie glanced in the direction indicated. The knife would have been ready to anyone's hand. He balanced the knife, considering the possibilities.

Kent Friede was dead, the body found by Jim Cane. Only a short time before, the two had almost come to blows before a dozen witnesses, and Friede had made his remark about wet stock. Bowdrie heard muttering in the gathering crowd, and Cane's name was mentioned.

Sheriff Hadley joined them. "This doesn't look good, Bowdrie. People are already complainin' that I haven't arrested Jim Cane for the bank robbery. Now this here is surely goin' to stir up trouble."

"Have you any evidence? Or have they? A lot of loose talk doesn't make a man guilty."

"No evidence I know of," Hadley agreed. "I'd never have suspected anything was wrong at the bank without you bringin' it up. What gave you the idea?"

"Tobacco smoke. Somebody was inside the bank before the outlaws got there. After tipping me off to the robbery and its time. Whoever it was figured I'd come a-shootin' and kill all or some of them and maybe get killed myself. In fact, I think he counted on that.

"Then during the gun battle outside he finished off the two inside and got away with the money. If I'd been killed too, there was just no way anybody could figure out what happened. He'd have the money and be completely in the clear."

"Looks like he is anyway," Hadley agreed ruefully. "This Friede, he might have known something."

"He knew a lot, a lot too much. You see, Sheriff, he knew who that other outlaw was. He knew the fifth man. He followed somebody to that outlaw camp and he crouched down in the mesquite and heard them planning it."

Bowdrie arranged for the body to be picked up and then walked back to the hotel, where he had taken a room. In the hotel he bundled the bedding together to resemble the body of a sleeping man; then he unrolled his blankets and slept on the floor.

The gun's report and the tinkle of falling glass awakened him. The bullet had smashed into the heaped-up clothing on the bed, then thudded into the wall. He got up carefully and eased to a position near the door. Outside somewhere a light went on and he heard an angry voice. He looked into the alley. It was dark, empty, and still.

He waited. A few people came out on the street, and he heard more complaints about drunken cowboys and disturbed sleep.

He studied the line the bullet must have taken to

break the window, penetrate the heaped-up bedding, and crash into the wall. It was, he reflected, the thud of the bullet into the wall that had awakened him, almost the instant of the report.

From beside the window he studied the situation. The bullet could have come from a dark corner of the livery stable, a place where a man might wait for hours without being seen. At night there was very little activity in town. Even the saloons closed by midnight.

Pulling on his clothing, he went into the street, moving toward the livery stable. The door gaped wide. There was a lantern hanging from a nail over the door, but nobody was around. A hostler slept in the tack room at the back of the stable during the busy times.

Stepping inside the door, he glanced around. He saw no cigarette butts, although when he squatted on his heels he detected a little ash. Taking a chance, he struck a match. There was some ash and a few fragments of tobacco. He scraped them together and put them in a fold of a sheet torn from his tally book.

Standing on the corner in the shadow of the barn, he saw he was no more than fifty yards from Jim Cane's cabin. He walked past the cabin, staying in the dust to make no sound. No light showed.

He walked past the sheriff's office and back to the hotel, passing the tree where young Tommy Ryan had been practicing throwing his knife.

Morning dawned bright and clear. Bowdrie went out into the street, feeling good. He knew the killer was both puzzled and worried.

A well-laid plan had backfired. Too many things had gone wrong, and now the killer did not know but what something else, something he had not thought of, might also have gone wrong. One way out remained. To kill Bowdrie. The Ranger knew more than he was expected to know and at any moment he might achieve a solution that would mean the collapse of all the killer's schemes and his own arrest.

That he had been marked for death on the day he rode into town, Bowdrie was well aware. That he survived the initial shoot-out had been the first thing to go wrong. Of course, even before that, Kent Friede had spied on the outlaw camp, but of that the killer had no knowledge at the time, and that situation had been remedied. Bowdrie remained.

He walked across the dusty street to the restaurant. Every sense was alert. What happened must take place within the next few hours. His hands were never far from the butts of his pistols. When he reached the restaurant door he looked around. Jim Cane stepped out of an alley and crossed the street toward him.

Bowdrie went inside and sat down. He knew the killer. He knew just who the other outlaw was and what he had done. The difficulty was that he had no concrete evidence, only several intangible clues, things that weighed heavily with him, but nothing he could offer a jury.

Jim Cane pushed open the door and strode across to his table. "How about the bank? Hadley says it's okay to open."

"How about a cup of coffee?" Bowdrie suggested. Then, as Cane seated himself, he added, "Sure, you can open up, and good luck to you. However"—he leaned closer—"you might do something for me." He went on, whispering.

Cane stared at him, then swallowed his coffee and left the café. Chick Bowdrie stirred his coffee and smiled at nothing.

Tommy Ryan came to the door and peered in; then he crossed to the table. "Mr. Bowdrie," he said, "I got somethin' to tell you. I seen who took my knife."

Bowdrie glanced at him sharply. "Who have you told besides me?"

"Nobody. On'y Pa. He said—"

"Tell me later. Why don't you sit over at that table, drink a glass of milk and eat a piece of that thick apple pie? On me."

Sheriff Hadley entered. He was a strapping big man and as usual he walked swiftly, his gray hat pulled down, the old-fashioned mule-ear straps flapping against the sides of his boots.

He dropped into the chair across from Bowdrie. "Bowdrie, I figured it only right to talk to you first. I got to make an arrest. It's no secret who done it. I've got to arrest a thief and a killer."

"Why not leave it to me?" His thick forearms rested on the table and his black eyes met those of the sheriff. "You see, I've known almost from the start who the guilty man was. Things began to tie up when I first saw those bodies lyin' on the floor in the bank. That dead outlaw? That was Nevada Pierce."

"Pierce? You sure of that?"

"Uh-huh. You see, I sent him to prison once. And his description was in the Rangers' Bible. Lots of descriptions there, Hadley."

Their eyes clung. "You mean . . . you got Jim Cane's description, too?"

"Sure. I spotted him right off. Jim used to run stock across the Rio Grande. That was four, five years ago."

"You knowed he was a horse thief and you haven't arrested him?"

"That's right, Hadley. You see, we live on the edge of lawless times. Lots of men got their first stake branding unbranded cattle. It surely wasn't theirs, but nobody else could prove a claim to it either. Afterward some other boys came along later, so to even things up, they switched brands.

"Now, maybe that's stealin', Hadley. By the book I guess it is. Nowadays it would surely be stealin', for there's no unclaimed stock runnin' around. It all belongs to somebody. It hasn't always been easy to decide who was a crook and who wasn't.

"So you know what I do? I judge a man by his record. Suppose a man who's rustled a few head in the old days goes straight after that? The country is settlin' down now, so if a man settles down an' behaves himself, we sort of leave him alone. If we went by the letter of the law, I could jail half the old-time cattlemen in Texas, but the letter of the law isn't always justice. It was open range then, and two-thirds of the beef stock a man could find was maverick. If a man goes straight, we leave him alone."

"What do you mean?" Hadley kept his voice low. "You call robbin' banks an' killin' goin' straight?"

"Not a bit of it. If Cane had robbed a bank or killed anyone, I'd have arrested him. He had nothing to do with it."

Their eyes met across the table and Bowdrie said, "That Rangers' Bible of ours, it carries a lot of descriptions, like I said. It has descriptions of all the crowd who used to run with Pierce.

"There was one thing always puzzled Pierce, and that was how the Rangers always managed to outguess him. What he never knew was that we were always tipped off by one of his own outfit."

Hadley pushed his chair back, both hands on the table's edge. "You've got this man spotted, Bowdrie?"

"Sure. He had a record, just like Cane, but at first I held off. Maybe I was prejudiced because of his record. It might have been Cane or Kent Friede, so I waited."

Chick Bowdrie lifted his coffee cup and looked over it at Sheriff Hadley. "You shouldn't have done it, Hadley. You had a nice job. People respected you."

"With eight thousand dollars just waitin' to be picked up? And Jim Cane to lay it on?" His tone deepened and became ugly. "An' I'd have made it but for you."

"You tipped the Rangers to that Pierce holdup, didn't you? We always wondered where the money got to. Now I know. The Rangers got him and you got the money, and now you've tried it again. You're under arrest, Hadley."

Hadley got to his feet, his hands hovering over his guns. "You make a move, Ranger, an' you die! You hear that?"

"Sure." Bowdrie still held his cup. "I hear."

Hadley backed through the door and ran across the street as Bowdrie got up and tossed a silver dollar on the table. "For the kid's grub, too," he said.

He glanced at the boy. "It was Hadley you saw, wasn't it?"

"Uh-huh. You lettin' him get away?"

"No, Tommy. I just didn't want any shooting in here. He won't get far, Tommy. You see, I planned it this way. There isn't a horse on the street, nor in the livery stable. Hadley won't go far this time."

Outside, the street was empty, yet people knew what was happening and they would be at the windows. Hadley was at his hiding place now, getting out the eight thousand dollars. Soon he would discover there was no horse in his stable, so he would rush to the street to get one.

"Only he knew where the money was, Tommy. The bank has to have it back. He'll get it for us."

Bowdrie walked outside and away from the front of the café.

Hadley emerged from an alley, a heavy sack in his hand, a pistol in the other. When he saw no horses tied at the hitching rails, he looked wildly about.

"Hadley, you needn't look. There ain't a horse within a quarter of a mile."

"You! You set me up!"

"Of course I did. Just as you set up your partners, time after time.

"I didn't have enough proof, Hadley. Only that there were no cigarette butts, just ashes and sometimes burned matches. You smoke a pipe, Hadley.

"Also, Pierce's old partner was a knife-thrower, and the knife that killed Friede had to be thrown. At first I thought he'd been killed elsewhere, because nobody could have walked up behind Friede over that gravel.

"We just had a few facts, Hadley, never a full description of you, so you could have gone straight and nobody the wiser. You tied it all up nicely, Hadley, you yourself."

Hadley's gun came up and Bowdrie drew and fired

before the gun came level. Flame stabbed from Bowdrie's pistol and the sheriff dropped the loot and tried to bring his gun into line. Something seemed to be fogging his vision, for when he fired again, he was several feet off the target.

Blood covered his shirt. He went to his knees. "A damn Ranger!" he said. Then he cursed obscenely. "It had to be a Ranger."

"Our job, Hadley, but you got yours in front, not in the back."

Hadley stared up at him; then his eyes glazed and the fingers on the pistol relaxed. Bowdrie bent down and took the gun from his fingers.

People came out on the street. Some lingered, shading their eyes to see. Others came closer. Bowdrie indicated the sack. "There's your money, Cane."

"Thanks. I moved the horses like you said." Then he asked, "How did you know?"

Bowdrie thumbed shells into his gun. He told Cane what he had told Hadley, then added, "It was all of it together, along with those mule-ear straps on Hadley's boots. I saw the marks on the sand made by them when he sat talking in the outlaw camp. Some of those old-timey boots like Hadley wore had loose straps to pull on the boots. Nowadays they make them stiffer and they don't dangle.

"I had an idea what might have made those marks, but when I saw Hadley, I knew. I had to be around town a mite to see if anybody else around was outfitted like him. Nobody was.

"All along, he had you pegged for the goat. He even rode one of your horses out there to talk to the outlaws. Hadley said he didn't know I was in the country, but I happen to know headquarters told him I was ridin' this way. He was the only one who could have thrown that note tipping me to the raid."

"You'd have thought he would have been sensible enough to go straight, with a good job, and all."

"Yeah," Bowdrie said, smiling at Cane, "the smart ones do go straight."

"You got time for something to eat? Mary Jane's frying up some eggs and she makes the best griddle cakes in Texas!"

"Home cookin'! I always did have a weakness for home cookin'. Although," Bowdrie added, "I never see much of it."

HISTORICAL NOTE:

HORSEHEAD CROSSING

In the days of westward travel the Pecos River was about one hundred feet wide and four feet deep at the Crossing's deepest. Such figures varied somewhat according to rainfall, of course, but rain was a rarity. There was nothing to indicate the presence of a river until one was close upon it. The riverbed lay eight to ten feet below the level of the surrounding prairie, and no trees marked its course.

The Crossing was named for the skulls of horses that lay about, said to be the remains of horses stolen by the Comanches, who ran them hard in escaping from Mexico. The horses, arriving at the first water in miles, drank too much. Rip Ford, Texas Ranger, is the authority for this story.

This was the crossing used by the Butterfield Stage. It was also used by a number of cattle drives, including that of Charlie Goodnight when he blazed the Goodnight-Loving Trail. Marcy was here in 1849, when exploring the westward route for the Army, and Bartlett, when he was surveying the U.S.-Mexican border.

Off to the west is El Capitan, over eight thousand feet high, a peak of the Guadalupes that was a noted landmark for travelers.

There were thirteen graves at Horsehead Crossing, most of them the result of gun battles between cowboys *over difficulties involved in making the crossing. Here, too, Hoy, with his wife, several cowhands, and a large herd, was attacked by Comanches. Several men were wounded, and the cattle stolen. The group took refuge in the ruins of the abandoned stage station, where they held off the Indians for days until rescued by a gold-hunting party led by Colonel Dalrymple.*

It was hot country; it was dry country; it was a country that was hell on horses and men. Patience was limited, and tempers short. It was a wonder there were not more graves at the Horsehead Crossing.

South of Deadwood

The Cheyenne to Deadwood Stage was two hours late into Pole Creek Station, and George Gates, the driver, had tried to make up for lost time. Inside the coach the five passengers had been jounced up and down and side to side as the Concord thundered over the rough trail.

The girl with the golden hair and gray eyes who was sitting beside the somber young man in the black flat-crowned hat and black frock coat had been observing him surreptitiously all the way from Cheyenne.

He had a dark, Indian-like face with a deep, dimplelike scar under his cheekbone, and despite his inscrutable manner he was singularly attractive. Yet he had not spoken a word since leaving Cheyenne.

It was otherwise with the burly red-cheeked man with the walrus mustache. He had talked incessantly. His name, the girl had learned with no trouble at all, was Walter Luck.

"Luck's my name," he stated, "and luck's what I got!"

The other blond was Kitty Austin, who ran a place of entertainment in Deadwood. Kitty was an artificial blond, overdressed and good-natured but thoroughly realistic in her approach to life and men. The fifth passenger had also been reticent, but it finally developed that his name was James J. Bridges.

"I want no trouble with you!" Luck bellowed. "I

don't aim to cross no bridges!" And the coach rocked with his laughter.

The golden-haired girl's name, it developed, was Clare Marsden, but she said nothing of her purpose in going to Deadwood until Luck asked.

"You visitin' relatives, ma'am? Deadwood ain't no place for a girl alone."

"No." Her chin lifted a little, as if in defiance. "I am going to see a man. His name is Curly Starr."

If she had struck them one simultaneous slap across their mouths they could have been no more startled. They gaped, their astonishment too real to be concealed. Luck was the first to snap out of it.

"Why, ma'am!" Luck protested. "Curly Starr's an outlaw! He's in jail now, just waitin' for the law from Texas to take him back! He's a killer, a horse thief, and a holdup man!"

"I know it," Clare said stubbornly. "But I've got to see him! He's the only one who can help me!"

She was suddenly aware that the dark young man beside her was looking at her for what she believed was the first time. He seemed about to speak when the stage rolled into the yard at Pole Creek Station and raced to a stop.

Peering out, they saw Fred Schwartz's sign—CHOICEST WINE, LIQUOR, AND CIGARS—as the man himself came out to greet the new arrivals.

The young man in the black hat was beside her. He removed his hat gracefully and asked, "If I may make so bold? Would you sit with me at supper?"

It was the first time he had spoken and his voice was low, agreeable, and went with his smile, which had genuine charm, but came suddenly and was gone.

"Why, yes. I would like that."

Over their coffee, with not much time left, he said, "You spoke of seein' Curly Starr, ma'am? Do you know him?"

"No, I don't. Only . . ." She hesitated, and then as he waited, she added, "He knows my brother, and he could help if he would. My brother is in trouble and I don't believe he's guilty. I think Curly Starr does know who is."

"I see. You think he might clear your brother?"

There was little about Curly Starr he did not know. Starr, along with Doc Bentley, Ernie Joslin, Tobe Storey, and a kid called Bill Cross had held up the Cattleman's Bank in Mustang, killing two men in the process. Billy Marsden, son of the owner of the Bar M Ranch, had been arrested and charged with the killing. It was claimed he was Bill Cross.

"I hope he will. I've come all the way from Texas just to talk to him."

"They'll be takin' him back to Texas," the young man suggested. "Couldn't you have waited?"

"I had to see him first! I've been told that awful gunfighting Ranger, Chick Bowdrie, is coming after him. He might kill Starr before he gets back to Texas."

"Now I doubt that. I hear the Rangers never kill a man unless he's shootin' at them. Have you ever met this Bowdrie fellow?"

"No, but I've heard about him, and that's enough."

Gates thrust his head in the door. "Time to mount up, folks! Got to roll if we aim to make Deadwood on time."

Clare Marsden hurried outside and Walter Luck stepped up beside her.

"Seen you talkin' with that young feller in the black hat. Did he tell you his name?"

"Why, no," she realized. "He did not mention it."

"Seems odd," Luck said as he seated himself. "We all told our names but him."

Kitty Austin drew a cigar from her bag and put it in her mouth. "Not strange a-tall! Lots of folks don't care to tell their names. It's their own business!"

She glanced at Clare Marsden. "Hope you don't mind the smoke, ma'am. I sure miss a cigar if I don't have one after dinner. Some folks like to chaw, but I'm no hand for it, myself. That Calamity Jane, she chaws, but she's a rough woman. Drives an ox team an' cusses like she means it."

Luck had a cigarette but he tossed it out of the window as the stage started.

The young man in the black hat reached into his pocket and withdrew a long envelope, taking from it a letter, which he glanced at briefly as they passed the last lighted window. He had turned the envelope to extract the letter, but not so swiftly that it missed the trained eye of Gentleman Jim Bridges. It was addressed, *Chick Bowdrie, Texas Rangers, El Paso, Texas*.

Bridges was a man who could draw three aces in succession and never turn a hair. He did not turn one now, although there was quick interest in his eyes. There was a glint in them as he glanced from Bowdrie to the girl and at last to Walter Luck.

"If you plan to see Starr, you'd better get at it," Luck suggested. "Texas wants him back and I hear they're sendin' a man after him. They're sendin' that border gunfighter, Chick Bowdrie."

"Never heard of him," Bridges lied.

"He's good, they say. With a gun, I mean. Of course, he ain't in a class with Doc Bentley or Ernie Joslin. That says nothin' of Allison or Hickok."

"That's what you say." Kitty Austin took the cigar from her teeth. "Billy Brooks told me Bowdrie was pure-Dee poison. Luke Short said the same."

"I ain't interested in such," Luck replied. "Minin' is my game. Or mine stock. I buy stock on occasion when the prospects are good. I don't know nothin' about Texas. Never been south of Wichita."

Bowdrie leaned back and relaxed his muscles to the movement of the stage. Clare Marsden aroused his sympathy as well as his curiosity, yet he knew that Billy Marsden was as good as convicted, and conviction meant hanging. Yet if his sister was right and Starr knew something that might clear him, he would at least have a fighting chance. How much of a chance would depend on what Starr had to say, if anything. The court would not lightly accept the word of an outlaw trying to clear one of his own outfit.

If he had even a spark of the courage it took to send his sister rolling over a thousand miles of rough roads, he might yet make something of himself.

Chick had himself made a start down the wrong road before McNelly recruited him for the Rangers. It had been to avenge a friend that he had joined the Rangers. It led to the extinction of the Ballard gang and the beginning of his own reputation along the border. Yet since he had ridden into that lonely ranch in Texas, badly wounded and almost helpless, he had never drawn a gun except on the side of the law.

It was easy enough for even the best of young men to take the wrong turning when every man carried a gun and when an excess of high spirits could lead to trouble. Chick Bowdrie made a sudden resolution. If there was the faintest chance for Billy Marsden, he would lend a hand.

Dealing with Curly Starr would not be simple. Curly was a hard case. He had killed nine or ten men, had rustled a lot of stock, stood up a few stages, and robbed banks. Yet so far as Bowdrie was aware, there were no killings on Starr's record where the other man did not have an even break. According to the customs of the country that spoke well for the man.

When the stage rolled to a stop before the IXL Hotel & Dining Room in Deadwood, a plan was shaping in Bowdrie's mind. He was the last one to descend from the stage and his eyes took in an unshaven man in miner's clothing who lounged against the wall of the IXL, a man who muttered something under his breath as Luck passed him.

Stooping, Bowdrie picked up Clare's valise with his left hand and carried it into the hotel. She turned, smiling brightly. "Thank you so much! You didn't tell me your name?"

"Bowdrie, ma'am. I'm Chick Bowdrie."

Her eyes were startled, and she went white to the

lips. He stepped back, embarrassed. "If there's any way I can help, you've only to ask. I'll be stayin' in the hotel."

He turned quickly away, leaving her staring after him.

Bowdrie did not wait to see what she would do or say, nor did he check in at the hotel. He had sent word to Seth Bullock, and knew the sheriff would have made arrangements. He headed for the jail.

Curly Starr was lounging on his cot when Bowdrie walked up to the bars. "Howdy, Starr! Comfortable?"

Starr glanced up, then slowly swung his feet to the floor. "Bowdrie, is it? Looks like they sent the king bee."

Bowdrie shook his head. "No, that would be Gillette or Armstrong. One of the others.

"Anyway, I've a lot of work to do when I get you back, Curly. There's Bentley, Joslin, Tobe Storey to round up." And then he added, "We've got the kid."

Starr came to the bars. "Got any smokin'?"

Bowdrie tossed him a tobacco sack and some papers. "Keep 'em," he said.

"Curly," he said as Starr rolled his smoke, "the kid's going to get hung unless something turns up to help him."

"Tough." Curly touched his tongue to the paper. "We can go out together, if you get me back to Texas."

"I'll get you back, settin' a saddle or across one, but that kid's pretty young to die. If you know anything that would help, tell me."

"Help?" Starr chuckled. He was a big, brawny young man with a hard, square brown face and tight dark curls. "You're the law, Bowdrie. You'd hang a man, but I doubt if you'd help one."

"He's a kid. I'd give any man a break."

"He was old enough to pack a gun. In this life a man straddles his own horses and buries his dead. Nobody is lookin' for any outs for me. Besides, how do I know you ain't diggin' for evidence against the kid? Or all of us?"

Despite himself Bowdrie was disturbed as he walked back to the IXL. He was positive the man Luck had spoken to was Tobe Storey. He had had only a glimpse, but the man's jawline was familiar, and the Pecos gunman could have ridden this way.

What if they had all ridden this way? What if they planned a jailbreak? Curly Starr was the leader of the outfit and they had ridden together for a long time.

Later, in the dining room of the IXL, he loitered over his coffee. Deadwood was wide open and booming. Named for the dead trees along a hillside above the town, it was really a succession of towns in scattered valleys in the vicinity.

The Big Horn Store, the Gem Theater, the Bella Union Variety Theater, run by Jack Langrishe, and the Number Ten Saloon all were busy, crowded most of the time.

After leaving the jail, Bowdrie had drifted in and out of most of the places, alert for any of the Starr outfit. Now he sat over coffee for the same purpose, waiting, watching.

The door opened and Seth Bullock appeared. With him was Clare Marsden. As her eyes met Bowdrie's, she flushed. Bowdrie arose as they came to the table.

"Bowdrie, this young lady wants to talk to Curly Starr. I told her Starr was your prisoner and she would have to ask you."

"She can talk to him," Bowdrie replied. From the corner of his eye he glimpsed a man standing just inside the saloon, looking into the dining room. It was the man he believed was Tobe Storey.

"Tonight?" Clare asked.

Bowdrie hesitated. It was foolhardy to open the jail now unless necessary, but . . .

"All right. I'll go along."

As she turned toward the door, he hesitated long enough to whisper to Seth Bullock, "Tobe Storey's in town, and maybe the rest of that Starr outfit."

She walked along beside him without speaking, until

suddenly she looked up at him. "I suppose you think I am a fool to come all this distance to help a man who is as good as convicted, even if he is my brother."

"No, ma'am, I don't. If you think there's a chance for him, you'd be a fool not to try, but if you've any reason for believing your brother wasn't involved, why not tell me?"

"But you're a *Ranger*!" The way she said it, the term sounded like an epithet.

"All the more reason. You've got us wrong, ma'am. Rangers don't like to jail folks unless they've been askin' for it. Out on the edge of things like this, if there weren't any Rangers there'd be no place for people like you.

"If your brother took money with a pistol, he's a thief and a dangerous man, and if he killed or had a part in killing an innocent man, he should hang for it.

"If he didn't, then he should go free, and if Starr has evidence that he's innocent, I'll do my best to clear him."

They turned a corner but a sudden movement in the shadows and the rattle of a stone caused Chick Bowdrie to swing aside, brushing Clare Marsden back with a sweep of his arm.

A gun flamed from the shadows and a bullet tugged at his shoulder. Only his sudden move had saved them, but his gun bellowed a reply.

He ran to the mouth of the alley, then stopped. It led into a maze of shacks, barns, and corrals, and there was nobody in sight. The ambusher was gone.

He walked back to Clare. She stared at him, pale and shocked. "That man tried to kill you!" she protested.

"Yes, ma'am. I am a Ranger and they know why I am in town."

"But why here? Deadwood is a long way from Texas!"

"I am here to take Starr back. They don't want him to go. If your brother was involved in that holdup, the man who tried to kill me is his friend. Or an associate, at least."

"My brother wouldn't do any such thing!" she protested, but her voice was weak.

He had expected something of the kind. His eyes narrowed thoughtfully as they neared the jail, remembering something he had noticed earlier.

The deputy on guard opened the door cautiously, gun in hand, then opened it wider when he saw who was there.

Starr was sprawled on his bunk. A big man in a checked shirt, jeans stuffed into cowhide boots.

He swung his feet to the floor. "You again? Was that you they shot at?"

"Wouldn't you know?" Bowdrie saw Starr's eyes go to the tear in the shoulder of Bowdrie's shirt. "Close, that one. I reckon the boys aren't holdin' as steady as they should."

His eyes shifted to Clare, and he came quickly to his feet, surprise mingled with respect. He could see at a glance that she was a decent girl, and he had that quick Western courtesy toward women. "How d'you do, ma'am?"

"Curly, this is Clare Marsden, sister of Billy Marsden. The law thinks he is Bill Cross. She hopes you can tell her somethin' that will get her brother off the hook."

Starr shrugged contemptuously. "Is this another trick, Bowdrie? I won't give evidence, not any kind of evidence. I don't know anybody named Marsden, or Cross either. I've nothing to say."

"You can't help me?" she pleaded. "If only Billy wasn't with you! Or if he was only holding the horses or something!"

Curly avoided her eyes. He looked a little pale but he was stubborn. "I don't know nothin' about it."

"You were seen an' identified by four men, Curly." Bowdrie's tone was gentle. "So was Tobe. Everybody in town knew Bentley. That leaves Joslin and the kid. We have no description of Joslin, but the kid was identified by one man and he was caught under suspicious circumstances. If you can save his neck, why not do it?"

She stared helplessly for a moment, then dropped her hands from the bars and turned away with a gesture of hopelessness that caught at Chick's heart.

"Starr, I knew you were a thief but I didn't think you were a damned louse! This won't do you any good."

"I'll do myself some good before we get to Texas. I'll have your hide, Bowdrie. It's a long road home and I'll get my break."

At the door of the IXL Bowdrie paused. "You'd best go home, ma'am. Most outlaws aren't like him. They are rough men but many of them are pretty decent at heart. I am sorry."

"Thank you, and I am sorry for what I said. You really tried to help me." Tears welled into her eyes and she turned away.

He stared after her, and swore under his breath.

The wind had a way of rippling the grass into long waves of gray or green, and it stirred now, rolling away over the sunlit prairie. Bowdrie, astride the appaloosa gelding he had bought in Deadwood, rode beside his prisoner.

Curly Starr, his chin a stubble of beard, stared bleakly ahead. "You won't get me much further! Ogalalla's ahead, an' I've friends riding the cattle trails."

"You talk too much. I've prob'ly just as many friends as you've enemies among those herds, too. You stole too many horses, Curly. I'll be lucky if I get you back to Texas unhung." He paused. "What happened to Tobe an' Doc?"

"How would they guess you'd ride fifty miles west out of Deadwood? That you'd ride fifty miles out of your way to keep me away from them? But you're back on the cattle trails now, an' they'll find us."

It had been a hard ride. On impulse Bowdrie had taken his prisoner out of Deadwood on the same night he left Clare Marsden at the door of the IXL. He headed due west, only later turning south and heading for the tall-grass country.

Ogalalla, which lay ahead, was a tough trail town and a dozen Texas herds were gathered nearby. Bowdrie had friends there, as did Starr. When things went well for him, the big outlaw was a friendly, easygoing man who had punched cows with many of the trail hands. Those friends would not forget.

Bowdrie kept his plans to himself. He had no intention of going into Ogalalla at all. He would camp at Ash Hollow, then head south again, keeping west of Dodge on a course roughly parallel to the proposed Nation Trail, until inside the Texas boundaries. At that time he would veer west toward Doan's Store and Fort Griffin.

"They'll be good hunters if they find us," Bowdrie commented. Starr looked at him, but said nothing. He had been watching the stars, and was puzzled.

At dusk they camped in a canyon where a few ash trees grew and which had been named Ash Hollow by Frémont. They made camp close to the spring, and then taking Starr with him, Bowdrie went down to a moist place in the brush where gooseberries and currants were growing. When they had picked a few to supplement their supper, they walked back.

"You takin' these irons off me? I'll sleep better if you do."

Bowdrie smiled. "And I'll sleep better with them on, so why don't you just settle down an' rest? Nobody is going to turn you loose unless you get a smart Texas lawyer."

Despite their continual bickering, the two men had come to respect and even like each other during the ride. Curly Starr was typical of a certain reckless, devil-may-care sort of puncher who often took to the bad trails when the country was wild. He was not an evil man, and under other circumstances in another kind of country he might never have become an outlaw.

Bowdrie was not fooled by his liking for the man. He knew that at the first chance Starr would grab for a gun or make a run for it. By now the outlaw knew something had gone awry with their planning. He kept staring around at the spring, then the ash trees.

"Hey?" he exclaimed. "This place looks like Ash Hollow, west of Ogalalla!"

"Go to the head of the class," Bowdrie replied.

"You're not goin' into Ogalalla?" Disappointment was written in his expression. "Ain't you goin' to give me any chance at all?"

"Go to sleep," Bowdrie said. "You've got a long ride tomorrow."

When he picketed the horses he took a long look around. Earlier he had glimpsed some distant riders who rode_like Indians.

He slept lightly and just before daybreak rolled out of his blankets and got a small fire going. Then he went for the horses. He was just in time to see an Indian reaching for the picket pin. The warrior saw him at the same instant and lifted his rifle. Bowdrie drew and fired in one swift, easy movement. Grabbing the picket ropes, Bowdrie raced back for the shelter of the trees.

Curly was on his feet. "Give me a gun, Bowdrie! I'll stand 'em off!"

"Lie down, Starr! If it gets rough I'll let you have a gun. In the meantime, just sit tight."

A bullet clipped a leaf over his head, another thudded into a tree trunk. Chick rolled into a shallow place in the grass and lifted his Winchester.

An instant he waited; then he glimpsed a brown leg slithering through the grass and aimed a bit ahead of it and squeezed off his shot. The Indian cried out, half arose, then fell back into the grass. A chorus of angry yells responded to the wounding of the warrior.

Bowdrie waited. This was, he believed, just a small party on a horse-stealing foray, and two of their number were down. His position was relatively good unless the Indians decided to rush them. Which they promptly did.

Dropping his rifle as they broke from the brush and arose from the grass, Bowdrie drew both six-shooters.

He opened fire, dropping the nearest Indian; then with his left-hand gun he got the man farthest on the right. Then they vanished, dropping into the grass and the brush. One warrior was slow in getting under cover and a rifle boomed behind Bowdrie and the Indian fell.

Bowdrie turned swiftly, covering Starr. The outlaw grinned at him. "Had to get in one shot!" he protested. Yet Bowdrie saw the man had started to swing the rifle to cover him. Only his quick turn with the pistol had stopped it.

He grinned again. "Hell, Bowdrie, you can't blame a man for tryin'!"

He nodded toward the area beyond their brush screen. "No real war party, just huntin' horses an' a few scalps."

An hour later they were on their way. It was short-grass country now and would be all the way back to Texas. There might be occasional belts of tall grass, but it was going to be scarce. Bowdrie kept them moving at a stiff pace, knowing Starr's followers would almost certainly figure out what had happened. He could not avoid them much longer.

Undoubtedly even now they were working their way west to cut his trail, and when they came, it would be fast.

When they did come, it was a surprise. Bowdrie had holed up in a deserted cabin in the upper Panhandle of Texas. Theirs had been a long, hard ride under blazing suns, cold nights, and sometimes showers of pounding rain. As they reached the cabin, Starr said, "You're goin' to a heap of trouble just to hang a man. Why don't you let me go?"

"Hangin' you isn't important," Bowdrie replied, "but I've got a job to do and you're part of it. The day has come when a man can no longer live by the gun. Two men were killed in that robbery of yours. Both of them had wives, one of them had two youngsters.

"Hangin' you won't bring back their father or that other woman her husband, but it might keep some other father or husband alive.

"Society is not taking revenge. It is simply eliminating someone who refuses to live by the rules."

Starr swore and spat into the dust. "Get me back to wherever you're takin' me, Bowdrie, or by the Eternal you'll have me converted! But keep them guns handy, boy. If I get a hand on one of 'em, I'll have a chance to be glad you aren't leavin' a widow!"

"Get busy an' pick up sticks. We'll need a fire for coffee."

On the edge of the hollow where the cabin lay, Chick paused and took a careful look at the surrounding country. His nerves were on edge, and in part it was due to the long ride with a man who was ready to kill him at any slight chance, a man with everything to gain and nothing to lose. Around the next hill or down the next draw his friends might be waiting.

Doc Bentley, Joslin, and the rest were all plainsmen and by now they would have figured out what he was doing and they would expect him to turn east, which he must do to deliver his prisoner. Also, they were on the edge of Kiowa-Comanche country.

Bowdrie studied the situation. The adobe cabin was built in a hollow in a rocky canyon with a spring close beside it. There were a few cottonwood trees, and a couple of huge tree trunks that lay near the cabin. The view from the door overlooked the trail and the approach to the spring. The cabin had often been a refuge for buffalo hunters and had figured in many a brush with Indians, judging by the bullet scars.

With an armful of wood on his left arm, Bowdrie walked back to the cabin. Working with the handcuffs on, Curly Starr had a fire going. He looked up, smiling.

"As long as they sent a Ranger after me, I'm glad they sent one who could cook. I believe I've gained weight on this trip."

Bowdrie built his fire of dry wood to eliminate smoke. Earlier, crossing the plains, he had killed an antelope. Now he cut steaks and began to broil them. He knew better than to relax.

"Always keepin' an eye out, aren't you?" Starr said. "I see you're pretty handy with a gun, too. You'll have to be if you ever tangle with Doc or Joslin.

"That Ernie's a pretty hand himself, you know. I had an idea he might try to cut me down someday. He wanted to boss the outfit himself, but he's too bloody.

"Between the two of us, it was Doc an' Joslin who did the killin'. I led them to that bank and I wanted the money, but I never figured on no killin'."

"Then why don't you give the Marsden kid a clean bill, Curly? He's young enough, an' he might turn into a pretty decent man."

"Or he might turn into a country lawyer." Starr glanced at him. "That pretty sister of his must have sold you a bill of goods."

A quail called out in the tall grass beyond the cottonwoods. There was a shade of difference in Starr's tone when he added, "She seemed like a mighty fine girl, at that."

Bowdrie was squatted beside the fire. His ear caught the change in Starr's tone. It had come right after that quail called. He pushed the coffeepot against the glowing sticks, pushed others closer.

He glanced around casually. Starr was sitting up more and he had drawn one foot back so the knee was bent and the foot was flat on the ground. His hands, still in the cuffs, lay loosely on his right side. At an instant's warning he could roll over and make a run for it.

Bowdrie's mind raced. His rifle was twenty feet away, leaning against the wall of the adobe cabin. He was between it and Starr. Starr's best bet if Bowdrie was attacked was to run for the shelter of the cottonwoods, climb a horse, and get out of there. As for himself, he would never make the cabin. He would have to fight it out right here, behind that log.

There was no sound but the bubble of coffee in the pot. He tossed Starr a cup. "Here!" he said.

Curly grabbed it but his eyes sparked. Bowdrie knew where they would be, among the cottonwoods. The toss of the cup had put Curly off guard, but for the moment only.

Curly had but one thing to do. To get away. Bowdrie had to both keep his prisoner and fight off three gunmen.

Bowdrie heard a rustle among the leaves and he turned, drawing as he wheeled. He fired into the brush from which the movement came, and as he fired Starr dropped his cup and lunged to his feet. Bowdrie had anticipated the move and he swung back and down with the barrel of his pistol, stretching Starr unconscious beside the fire.

Bowdrie dropped behind the log and snapped a quick shot at a stab of flame from the brush. Rolling over, he crawled the length of the log, getting closer to the doorway and his rifle.

"Hold it, Bowdrie!" a voice called. "Turn Starr loose an' you can ride off!"

It was the moment he wanted, for they would be listening for his reply and not poised to shoot. With a lunge he was through the door and inside the adobe house. Two bullets struck the doorjamb as he went through.

"You boys come in with your hands up," he called, "and I'll see you get a fair trial!"

"You're a fool!" somebody grumbled. "You haven't a chance. We'll burn you out!"

"Anytime you're ready!"

The fire was blazing brightly and to approach the cabin they must make a frontal attack. He reached around the doorpost and got his Winchester.

In the corner of the adobe was a huge pile of sticks, part of it a pack rat's nest, part of it wood for the fireplace, left by nameless travelers. Taking up one of the sticks, he tossed it into the fire. As the fire blazed up, he detected a slight movement from Curly Starr.

"Curly," he spoke loud enough for the outlaw to hear, "don't make any sudden moves. If you try to escape, I'll kill you. I don't want to, so don't push your luck."

He waited, and all was still. Nobody wanted to rush him as long as the fire was burning brightly. He threw another stick into the fire. In the next half-hour three of the five sticks he threw landed in the fire. Yet it was a long time until morning.

Starr had witnessed the brief battle with the Indians and had no idea of taking the risk. He reached for the coffeepot, snared it and a cup, and calmly filled the cup.

"Thanks, Bowdrie. All the comforts of home!"

"I should have hit you harder," Chick replied cheerfully. "You've a thick skull."

"You hit me hard enough. My head feels all lopsided. Why don't you be smart and turn me loose?"

"They'd kill you," Chick said.

"Kill *me*? Are you crazy?"

Although the outlaws could hear him talking, they would not be able to distinguish the words.

"When the shootin' was goin' on, one of the bullets was aimed for you. Missed by mighty little."

"You're lyin'! Doc an' Tobe are my friends!"

"What about Joslin?"

Curly Starr was silent.

After a while he threw another stick into the fire and somebody shot at him, but the bullet was high. Later, he glimpsed the flickering light from a fire back in the trees, sixty or seventy yards away.

Starr spoke suddenly. "Did you mean that? About the shot?"

"It hit the log right over you, and couldn't have been aimed at me."

Bowdrie waited, studying the fire. He could barely see it flickering but decided to take a chance. Lifting his rifle, he fired three quick shots. He was shooting through underbrush which might deflect a bullet, but at least one shot got through. Sparks shot up from the fire and somebody swore.

Later, he must have dozed, because he awakened

with a start. Undoubtedly the outlaws were waiting until morning, not relishing an attack past the firelight.

Bowdrie crawled to the hole where the spring was. The old gourd dipper was probably dusty, but . . . He dipped up water and poured some over his head, then dipped again and drank.

The spring was right outside the wall, but the first resident or someone later had removed adobe bricks so the spring could be reached without going outside in case of an Indian attack. Suddenly Bowdrie got out his knife and began digging at a brick beside the hole. Carefully he removed several of the crumbling adobe bricks. Then he tossed a couple of sticks on the fire.

Returning, he slipped through the hole and flattened against the rock wall beyond the spring. He waited, but nothing moved.

Placing each foot with care, he moved away from the house. By the time he was close to the fire the sky was growing gray. One man was asleep, the other was placing fuel under the coffeepot. He was about to step out when the sleeping man opened his eyes and got to his feet suddenly. His eyes focused on Bowdrie, realization hit him, and he gave a startled yip and went for his gun. Bowdrie fired, but the man was weaving and his bullet missed.

A bullet whipped past his face, another hit his holster, half-turning him with its force. He fired again and Doc Bentley fell back against a tree.

Bowdrie swung his gun to Tobe, who, startled by Doc's surprised move, had shot too fast. Bowdrie's bullet caught Tobe Storey in the middle of the stomach and he stepped back and sat down. He started to lift his gun but could not. He fell sidewise and lay on his shoulder against the ground.

Bowdrie swung on Doc but the gunman lifted a shaky left hand. "Don't shoot! I've had it."

"Throw your gun over here. With your left hand."

The gun landed at his feet. "Where's Joslin?"

Doc made a feeble gesture with his left hand and,

thumbing shells into his right-hand gun, Bowdrie ran into the woods. Suddenly he heard an outburst of firing at the cabin.

Ducking through the woods, he ran up to the fire. Ernie Joslin was standing over the fire. He was unsteady on his feet but he held a gun.

He turned toward Bowdrie, lifting his gun. Bowdrie fired. Joslin stood for an instant, then fell flat, all in one piece. Bowdrie walked over to him and kicked the gun from his hand.

Joslin was staring at him, his face against the ashes and earth. "If I'd known who you was there at first—"

"I knew who you were. I knew you by the cigarette. You threw it away too late. You said you'd never been south of Wichita, but folks around Deadwood don't smoke cigarettes. It's a Mexican habit, although it's workin' its way north, I expect. Men up Dakota, Montana way smoke cigars. Up north they think cigarettes are kind of ladylike."

He turned to Starr. "Take off . . . take off these damned cuffs," Starr pleaded. "I don't want to die with 'em on."

Starr coughed, and when the coughing was over and the cuffs were off, he asked, "You got him?"

"One of us did."

Folding his coat, he placed it under the head of the dying man. Then he opened Starr's shirt. There was nothing he could do.

"Got to your pack. Seen where you put my guns. I was figurin' on a break when Joslin come for me. He killed those men back yonder. Him an' Doc. I never went for killin' m'self. Joslin, he was a bad one. I knowed he didn't like me much, but . . ."

For a long time he was silent and then he whispered, "You write it. The boy . . . You say Bill Cross is gone. Dead. Buried. Put . . . it down."

Billy Marsden was not in my outfit. The man named Bill Cross was badly wounded and we bur-

*ied him in the hills. The killing was done by Ernie
Joslin and Doc Bentley. This is my dying statement.*

Bowdrie wrote it, then read it to him. "Good!" He
waited, gathering strength, then he signed his name.
"You . . . you keep that kid . . . straight."

Bowdrie put wood on the fire. A glance at Joslin told
him the man was gone. He hesitated to leave Starr, but
he went back through the patch of woods.

As he came through the woods, he heard a shot. He
hesitated, then went on. Tobe Storey lay where he had
fallen.

Doc Bentley lay nearby. His right hand was horribly
mangled from a bullet. He had taken Tobe's gun and
shot himself.

"Maybe it's better than hangin'," Bowdrie said aloud;
then, gathering up the weapons, he walked back to
Starr.

"Joslin never liked me." Starr had wiped the blood
from his face and had pulled himself into a sitting
position. "Figured to have all that bank loot for himself.
It's cached under a flat rock at Granite Spring."

He lay quite awhile, then said, "That Marsden girl?
Sure pretty, wasn't she?" His voice trailed off and then
he said, "Chick? Bury my saddle with me, will you?
Might have some mean broncs where I'm goin'. Man
feels the need of . . . of his own . . . saddle."

"Want your boots off?"

There was a flicker of a smile on Curly's lips. "Lived
with 'em on. I'll die with 'em, only don't cache me with
him. Not with Joslin."

Bowdrie went for the horses and brought them in,
and loaded them with the weapons of the fallen men.
Suddenly he heard Starr choking and ran to him. He
had thrown out a hand and was gripping the horn of his
saddle as it lay on the ground.

"They got me, kid! Bowdrie . . . I'm pullin' leather!"

Bowdrie dropped beside him and put a hand on

Starr's shoulder. His hand had been there for several minutes before he realized the man was dead.

In the cool of the morning with the sun on his shoulders, Chick Bowdrie headed south and east, carrying in his thoughts the memory of a man who died game, and in his pocket another man's chance for a new life.

HISTORICAL NOTE:

DOAN'S STORE

At the crossing of the Red River on the Western Trail from San Antonio to Fort Griffin to Dodge City, stood a place established by Corvin F. and Jonathan Doan. It was a rude, hastily thrown together structure of pickets with a mud and brush roof and a flapping buffalo hide for a door. Later, when time permitted, an adobe store was built to handle the increasing trade as the cattle trails shifted west.

This was the last place at which even the most limited supplies could be purchased. North lay Indian Territory and the long dusty drive to Dodge. A few miles south lay Eagle Flat, where cattle were rounded up before the final drive north.

Later, a dozen houses were built in the area, as was a hotel called The Bat's Cave.

Doan's Store and Crossing was known to every cattleman and trail driver, and it is said that somewhere between six and seven million head of cattle were driven over the Western Trail and crossed the Red at Doan's Store. From there it was roughly three hundred miles to Dodge.

During the great days of the cattle drives, nearly every trail driver of note rode this trail, as they had ridden those further east.

Had they kept a register, it would have held the names of most of those famous or infamous who traveled the wild country.

The Outlaws of
Poplar Creek

Moby Fosdick kept the trading post at Lee's Canyon, and Moby was a hard man. It took a man with a cold eye and a ready hand to do business in the Poplar Creek country, and Moby had been there a long time.

The store was a low-roofed building built in a hollow of the hills just below the falls of Poplar Creek. Lee's Canyon, narrow and rock-walled, was mostly uphill until within two hundred yards of the trading post. Then it topped a rise and the trail slid down into the hollow with a creek to the north.

From the store you could hear the roar of the falls, perhaps a quarter of a mile away.

If you just rode up to the post, did your buying and then rode away, you would believe there was only one way in and one way out, both along the Lee's Canyon trail.

A knowing man could tell you there were at least two other trails out of the hollow and into the badlands. One led through a crevice in the rock wall, invisible until close up, an opening that barely allowed room for a man on a horse. If it were a heavy horse, the rider might have to push one stirrup well forward to slip through.

Across the wide spread of Poplar Creek the rock wall

reared up for about three hundred feet, but downstream there was a gravel beach perhaps ten feet long.

Moby had often wondered about that beach. He was an old Indian fighter with an eye for terrain, and it looked like water had been running down through some crack in the wall after heavy rains, but no opening could be seen.

Moby planned to someday build a boat and have a look over there. If there was an opening it would be another way out. Busy around the place and with occasional customers, he just never found the time, but it lingered there, in the back of his mind.

The second of the unseen paths was up the face of the cliff itself, the trail beginning among some poplars across the hollow and maybe a half-mile from the post. It wound up the cliff, always hidden behind juniper and ponderosa pine.

Fosdick knew the trails, and the wild bunch knew them. At the head of the cliff trail on a little plateau there was a cave. Once, during an Indian attack when Jerry and Lily Fosdick were youngsters, they had holed up there with Moby and two other men until the attack was over.

Moby had windows overlooking the trail from either side, and nobody could enter the hollow without being seen. So when the rider on the strawberry roan topped the rise from Del Rio, he saw him.

His hard old eyes narrowed with speculation as they watched the shambling, loose-gaited stride of the roan. The rider was a stranger.

Few travelers came by way of Lee's Canyon, and most sought to avoid it. Nobody knew where the Tucker gang holed up, but there were rumors. Fosdick knew the wild bunch but he also knew most of the hands who worked on ranches west of him. The rider wearing the black flat-crowned hat was nobody he remembered seeing before.

Fosdick strode to the door and shaded his eyes against the setting sun. The trail was empty. He looked off to the south and the hidden road. Nobody there, either. The stranger was drawing near.

Moby took in the dark, Indian-like face and the two guns. Not many men carried two guns in sight. A lot of them had a hideout. He glanced at the rider's face as he stepped down from the saddle. There was something about that still, emotionless face that gave him a little chill.

He had known this time would come and now he had a decision to make. He had expected it would come with a dozen hard-riding men, not a lone horseman on a wicked-looking hammerhead roan. He looked again. That was probably the ugliest, meanest-looking horse he had ever seen.

"Howdy! How about some grub?"

"Come in! Come in! Lily, set another place. We've got company!"

Fosdick turned back to the rider. "You can wash up right outside the door there. Fresh towel an' soap. Put it out m'self, not an hour ago." He glanced at the roan. "I'll take your hoss around an' give him some hay." He paused. "Shall I take the hull off him or will you be ridin' on?"

"If you've room, I'll stay the night." The rider looked at Moby. "Treat that horse gentle-like, and be careful. He both kicks and bites on occasion. Give him the hay first so he'll know you're friendly."

Fosdick walked to the barn with the roan. Well, that settled it. Hell would break loose now and Jerry would be caught right in the middle. To protect his son he would have to warn the whole Tucker gang.

Jake Rasch was standing in the shadows of the stable. His greasy, unshaved face was suspicious. "Who's that in yonder? I seen him ride up an' figured I'd better play possum."

"Hit the trail, Jake. You get to Shad Tucker as quick as you can make it. Tell him there's a traveler down here who looks like a Ranger, and he looks pretty salty."

"One man?" Rasch sneered. "What's one Ranger goin' to do with all of us? Even with one of us?"

"You ain't seen him," Fosdick said dryly. "This gent's got the bark on! Rough! I can tell! You look into those black eyes and it's like lookin' into two six-shooters with the hammers drawed back."

Jake's expression changed. He grabbed Fosdick's arm. "Black eyes! Looks like an Apache?"

"That's him." Fosdick lifted the saddle from the roan's back and set it astride a rail. "What's the matter?"

"*Chick Bowdrie!*" Jake's face paled with excitement. "He's the one cleaned up the Ballard outfit!"

Resolution came to Fosdick. "Jake, you tell Jerry to meet Lily at the cave at sunup tomorrow. I've got word for him. Now, don't forget!"

"All right," Rasch said. "Bowdrie, huh? If I could only git him!"

"Are you crazy?" Fosdick's contempt was poorly concealed. "If you're smart you'll just forget that. You never saw the day you could match Clyde Ballard, and he wasn't good enough."

"I wasn't thinkin' of givin' him no even break. He's after us, ain't he?"

To kill Chick Bowdrie! As Rasch rode up the cliff trail, he sat hunched in the saddle dreaming of what it would mean. Why, he'd become one of the most famous men in the border country! In all of Texas! And to Jake Rasch Texas was the world.

There'd be nobody to say how it was done. That girl in El Paso, she'd sure set up an' take notice of him if he got Bowdrie.

Three men lay about the fire at Cedar Springs when Jake Rasch returned to camp. Shad Tucker was a big, rawboned young man with features that betrayed the ugly savagery that lay beneath the surface. In a dozen years of outlawry he had come off scot-free in his brushes with the law. He claimed to have killed twenty men. Actually he had killed twelve, only three of whom had had an even break.

He was brutal, ignorant, and disdainful of the law.

"What's up?" he demanded, recognizing the excitement in Jake Rasch.

"Chick Bowdrie's down at the post. He's stayin' the night."

"Bowdrie?" His eyes turned mean as he saw the sudden apprehension in Buckeye Thomas's face. "If 'n he's huntin' us, he's askin' for it!"

"Stay shy of him," Frank Crowley advised.

Tucker spat. "He ain't so much! It's time somebody showed this Bowdrie a thing or two."

"Whar-at is Jerry Fosdick? I got word from the old man. He wants Jerry to meet Lily at the cave tomorrow at sunup."

Shad Tucker looked around at him. "You don't need to tell Jerry nothin'. I'll go to the cave."

Buckeye laughed coarsely and Jake's eyes showed his envy. Crowley looked up.

"You think that's wise, Shad? The old man's been a help, time an' again."

"He won't be no more. I been suspicious of him, an' he never wanted Jerry to tie up with us. I reckon it's time we cleaned up Fosdick. We'll take his money and the gal and we'll git all he has in that store. He's got a rifle or two I've had my eyes on for months."

Crowley knew Shad Tucker hated Fosdick because he sensed the contempt Fosdick had for him.

"We'll send Jerry off somewheres an' tell him the Rangers done it."

They all knew about the iron box under the floor.

"Might as well git on with it. Jake, you go down there an' kill Fosdick. You can git him through a window. Then git back here. We'll handle that Bowdrie when he trails after you."

Jake Rasch's face was sweaty. He was chewing on a chunk of beef. "Better wait until mornin'," he advised. "Give Lily a chance to start for the cave."

*   *   *

Back in Lee's Canyon Bowdrie accepted another plate of *frijoles* and cornbread. Lily, a slender, pretty blond girl, filled his cup with fresh coffee. "You're not very talkative, Mr. Bowdrie," she said, smiling.

"No, ma'am, I guess I'm not rightly a talking man. I've got lots of figurin' to do. Anyway," he added, "I know more about horses than folks, and the folks I know are mostly the bad ones. Gives a man a jaundiced opinion, I'm afraid."

"Don't you have a family?"

"No, ma'am. Once, when I was a youngster, but that's a long time ago. I went to work soon's I was able. Never had much time to get acquainted, me bein' out with stock all the time."

"Don't you have a girl?"

"No, ma'am. I've knowed a few here an' there, but there's not been many where I was. I don't even have one to dream about. There was a girl out in Tascosa, she was married to an Irish gambler, an' many's the cowpuncher rode miles just to look at her, she was that beautiful. I never rode that way when she was around."

He did have figuring to do. Fosdick had been too long taking care of the roan. Had there been somebody else out there? And where was young Jerry? At this time of night he should have been around.

Fosdick had looked anxious and irritated about something, and then Bowdrie heard somebody riding away. The horse did not go east or west or he would have heard the hoofbeats on the hard trail. He had heard three, maybe four hoofbeats, which meant the rider had crossed the trail, not ridden along it. The rider had ridden toward that apparently impassable wall of cliffs.

His deductions were wrong in one instance. Knowing Fosdick had a son, he assumed the rider was Jerry. Obviously he would be riding to warn the Tuckers, which implied a friendly relationship. Yet when Fosdick returned to the table Bowdrie could not reconcile the man's manner or his personality with what he knew of the Tuckers.

Chick Bowdrie's arrival was no accident. Tucker's gang had made a brief foray into Mexico, killing three people, one of them a woman, and stealing a bunch of horses. The Mexican government complained and McNelly sent Bowdrie to investigate.

So far the Tucker outfit had been confining their activities to the wilder, less-known areas, but emboldened by success, they had been striking at larger, richer places.

Getting a map of Texas, Bowdrie made ink marks to indicate the locations of the various raids. Then he calculated a probable location of their hideout as the various robberies seemed to radiate out from a given center, which could be Lee's Canyon. He had checked out several badland locations before coming to Fosdick's trading post.

Nobody had wanted to talk about the rough country south of Poplar Creek, although willing enough to talk of other places, so he deduced his search must begin there.

He took it for granted there was some kind of a working agreement or truce between the Tucker outfit and Fosdick. Otherwise he could not have existed there.

Obviously both Fosdick and Lily were disturbed by his presence. Shad Tucker would know Bowdrie was here and would resent his presence. So while he ate, he listened, every sense alert. Outside a coyote was howling.

Bowdrie was finishing his coffee when the coyote stopped howling. No coyote stopped howling suddenly on a moonlit night without reason. Somebody or something had disturbed that coyote. Chick lifted a forkful of beans, his dark eyes intent and aware. Lily's eyes were large and her lower lip was caught under her teeth.

Her brother? Or someone else? Chick's eyes sought her face, watching her expression. She had lived here, she knew the night sounds better than he. In that instant Jake Rasch's face appeared at the window. Neither Bowdrie nor Lily saw him, but Jake glimpsed the room, seeing what he wished to see.

Chick Bowdrie sat with his back to the door. Opposite him sat Moby Fosdick, and with luck Jake could get them both. His footsteps were catlike as he approached the door.

His heart was jumping like mad. It was the chance of a lifetime! To the devil with Tucker. If he could kill Bowdrie he'd be a big man, bigger than Tucker, and he could always tell Shad he just had to kill him. Yet Bowdrie's reputation was such that when Jake's hand touched the latch, it was trembling.

Six-gun gripped in his hand, he gripped the door latch with his left, and slamming the door back, he fired two quick shots into *an empty space*!

In the moment when Jake was rounding the corner of the house, Bowdrie got up and stepped to the corner for his saddlebags and Fosdick leaned over to get a light from the fire for his pipe.

Tense, every nerve on edge, Jake had fired at the place where the two men had been sitting. Only then did he realize they were gone. Pale with shock and sudden fear, he swung the gun, looking for Bowdrie.

Chick was standing, his saddlebags in his left hand, his gun in his right. He was standing casually, eyes alert, staring at Rasch.

The outlaw gulped, the sound loud in the room. The old clock ticked twice while horror mounted in Jake's breast. He found himself in the last situation he wanted to be in, facing Chick Bowdrie with an even break.

"Well"—Bowdrie was cool—"you came to kill me. Why don't you shoot?"

Transfixed with fear, Rasch forgot the girl in El Paso. He forgot about the important man he wanted to be. Suddenly the cost was enormously large. His mouth opened and closed. He tried to swallow. "You . . . you'd kill me! I wouldn't have a chance!"

"How much chance were you givin' us?"

Jake Rasch let his tongue touch his lips. Lust to kill was mounting past his fear. He took a step back toward the door, then another. Bowdrie's eyes were on him.

"No," he whined. "I was a fool! I was—"

He turned toward the door, then fired suddenly across his chest.

Bowdrie had been watching with the eyes of experience. The treachery in the man was obvious. He could see the fever to kill in the man's eyes. His gun was ready, and when he saw the man's knuckle move, his thumb on the hammer, Bowdrie killed him.

Jake's gun blasted, and there was a thud in the wall behind him. The gun slipped from Rasch's fingers and his legs seemed to melt under him. He sank to the floor, half in, half out of the door.

Moby Fosdick stared at the fallen man, then at the groove cut by Rasch's bullet in the surface of the table. Had he not leaned to pick that twig from the fire, he would be dead.

He realized what a fool he had been. There could be no tolerating of evil. One stamped it out or the evil grew worse. He had held on, hoping the Tuckers would leave the area or be killed. Now he knew that not only himself but his son and daughter were in danger.

"Lily, pack your things. Come daybreak we're gettin' out of here."

"Who was he?"

"Jake Rasch. He rides with Tucker."

Bowdrie knew the name. He was on the list of wanted men. "Who did he want? You or me?"

"I don't know." He looked at the groove again. "Looks like he wanted me, probably both of us."

Daylight was filtering into the hollow when Bowdrie rolled out of the hay, left the stable, and walked toward the house. A paint horse stood head down at the hitching post. Bowdrie considered it, reaching some agreement with himself. He was turning toward the door when it opened softly. Quickly he flattened himself against the wall and in the shadows of a tree.

Lily Fosdick slipped from the door, glanced fearfully toward the stable where she thought him to be, then hurried away across the clearing. Without stirring, he watched her enter the cedars near the cliff.

Moby was stirring around inside when Bowdrie entered. "Got some coffee on," he suggested. "Better have some."

"I'm going after the Tuckers this morning. Got anything you want to tell me?"

Moby straightened up from the fire. "I guess . . . not. They've got them a hideout, can't be more'n five or six miles off, the way they come an' go."

Bowdrie gulped hot black coffee and waited. Something was worrying Fosdick.

"Bowdrie, you've got a name for killin' men, but they say you're square. My boy's out there, Bowdrie. He ain't a bad boy, but it got kind of lonesome here and those fellers talked big about all they done. He sort of took up with Tucker. I don't reckon he's done anything wrong yet, ain't been time, and they ain't been away, so—"

"Any boy can get into trouble. No reason he has to keep on that road. I had a start that way myself but turned off before it was too late. As for killin', I don't do any more than I have to. Rasch there, he gave me no choice."

When Bowdrie had the saddle on the roan, he tied the reins of the paint horse to the saddle horn and said, "Go home, boy. You go home now."

The paint hesitated, trotted off a few steps, then headed down the trail. Whether the gelding understood or not, he remembered where the other horses were and where he'd been fed and watered.

There was no sign of Lily. He saw her tracks, then lost them as he followed the paint.

Almost an hour later Shad Tucker got up from the fire and saw the paint come trotting into the clearing. He stiffened, eyes narrow. "Frank? Look there!"

Crowley stood up. "Looks like Jake made a bad mistake," he commented dryly.

"Hey?" He dove into the brush, reaching for his rifle as he passed the rock where he had been sitting. "See those reins? Tied to the horn. I betcha that Ranger's followin'."

A short distance back along the trail, Bowdrie was puzzled. There should be some smoke. At this time of the morning somebody would be making coffee. He saw the paint had pulled up near a corral where there were other horses. He turned to look toward the left and saw the fire. He also saw two rifle barrels, and they were pointed at him.

"Jest set right still, Ranger. An' keep both hands on the pommel."

Chick Bowdrie swore softly. It would be madness to move now. At that distance they could not miss.

Shad Tucker came out of the brush. Behind him was Buckeye Thomas. "Good man, Frank!" Tucker said. "We got him dead to rights!"

Thomas bared his yellow teeth. "The great Chick Bowdrie! Wal, Mr. Ranger, I reckon you got to be taught. I reckon so."

Tucker gestured at the maze of canyons and rough country. "This here's mine! You Rangers ain't needed. We'll just sort of make an example of you an' leave what's left for Rangers to find so they'll know what's comin' to 'em if they come into my country."

"There will be others," Bowdrie said calmly. "Others who are tougher and smarter than me."

"When they find you," Tucker replied, "they'll find you with no hands, nor will you have any eyes or skin on your chest. I'll keep you alive for all o' that, then leave what's left to the ants and the buzzards."

Crowley glanced from one to the other, worry in his eyes. Bowdrie could see that Crowley didn't like it. Robbery and killing was one thing, torture something else. "Shad, Lily will be down to the cave about now, won't she?"

Tucker slapped his thigh. "Damned if she won't! I

almost forgot. I figured to keep that appointment she made with Jerry, so I better get down there."

Tucker reached up and flipped Bowdrie's guns from their holsters; then, grabbing him by the shirtfront, he jerked him from the saddle and threw a wicked punch to his belly. "How d'you like it, Ranger? You think you're tough, huh? Well, we'll see."

When Bowdrie was bound hand and foot, Shad Tucker swung to the saddle of his own horse and started down the trail. "Hold him for me. Don't do nothin' until I git back. This one's my meat."

"What about Jerry?"

"If he shows up, keep him here. Lily"—he grinned—"will be surprised to see me, but she'll get used to it."

Crowley looked down at Bowdrie. "You'd be dead if I had my way. This other idea is Shad's."

He walked to the fire and leaned his rifle against a log while he poured a cup of coffee.

Bowdrie, left alone for a moment, studied his situation with no pleasure. He was propped in a sitting position against a log, hands tied behind him, ankles bound together. Thomas was sprawled on a blanket across the fire, Crowley sipping coffee. The stump of a huge tree stood near Chick. In its edge were numerous gashes where an ax had been struck.

He heard the approaching horse several minutes before either of the others. The rider rode into the clearing, a clean-cut young man of nineteen with quick, nervous movements but a steady gray eye that Bowdrie instinctively liked.

"Snoopin' Ranger. Ketched him easy. Name of Bowdrie."

"Bowdrie?" Jerry Fosdick turned to look. "I've heard of him." He paused. "If you see Shad tell him I'm goin' down to the post to see Pa."

"You're to stay here," Thomas said. "Shad wants you here until he gits back."

Bowdrie had done what he wanted with his feet. He looked over at Jerry. "Tucker's gone to the cave to be alone with your sister. She thinks she's meeting you there. And Jake Rasch tried to kill your pa last night. Now Jake's dead. I killed him."

Buckeye jumped to his feet. "That's a damn lie!"

"Hold it!" Jerry's face was pale. "You said Lily thinks she's meetin' me? That Shad's gone down there?"

"Set down, kid." Thomas tried to be casual. "Ain't nothin' to it."

"Then why are you tryin' to stop me from goin' down there?" He swung his horse and Thomas dropped a hand to a gun. "You stay here, kid. When Shad wants him a woman, nobody butts in!"

Bowdrie had wedged a spur into a crack in the stump; he gave a quick jerk on the foot and it slipped from the boot. He lunged to his feet and threw himself at Crowley's back. The lunge sent Crowley sprawling against Thomas, and they both fell.

"Cover them, kid! Then cut my hands loose!"

Crowley, who had gotten up, dove into the brush. Jerry followed him with a quick shot; then, catching up a knife lying near the fire, he cut Bowdrie's hands loose. Chick grabbed up his guns, pulled on his boot, and ran for the roan.

"You watch him, kid! If he makes a wrong move, kill him! I'm goin' after your sister."

"I'm goin' too!"

"You stay here!"

Lily had waited anxiously, and when she heard the approaching horse, she stepped out of the cave. When she saw who it was, she drew back quickly, but not quickly enough. It was the first time she had seen Tucker when her father was not present. "Oh, I thought it was Jerry."

Shad hung a leg around the saddle horn and began building himself a smoke. He could see the mounting fear in her eyes and it was like wine in his blood. "You can quit expectin' him. I come instead."

"You mean . . . he's been hurt?"

"He don't even know you're here. I figured it would be more fun if I came alone. Anyway, I'm takin' you with us. Gits lonesome over in the badlands with no woman around."

"I'm going back to the post!" Lily said. "I'll see my father about this!"

Tucker dropped his foot back in the stirrup and brought his horse in front of her. "Jest sit tight, filly! We got business to do after I finish my smoke. You don't want your pa killed, do you?"

"Killed? Oh, you wouldn't dare!"

"Kill him? I aim to. He figures hisself too high an' mighty to suit me. As for that Ranger, don't you go to thinkin' he'll help. We got him back to camp, all tied up for skinnin'."

He swung down from his horse and tied it to a bush with a slip knot. Cut off from the trail, there was only one way for her to move. She darted into the cave.

She heard Shad's brutal laughter. "Like the dark, do you? I'll be right in!"

She stopped, looking around. It was even worse in the cave. Yet suddenly she remembered the opening she and Jerry had found. She ran on, stumbling in the dark. Behind her Shad Tucker's boots grated on rock.

Horror choked her. Behind her was Shad, his leering unshaved face, his broken-nailed hands. She ran into the dark. Then she could no longer run, for the floor was covered with fallen rock. She felt her way to the wall, waiting, thinking.

This cave had never been fully explored. She and Jerry had planned it, and had prepared torches for the purpose. Behind her, Tucker was fumbling about, growing more and more angry because of the trouble she was causing. He found a pile of the torches and lit one. The reflected light helped her.

She went on into an almost square room. The only escape was a dark opening, scarcely more than a crack, in the wall opposite. She paused, panting from her running and the close air. She went through the crack, and paused in amazement; the faint reflection from behind her seemed to touch upon a forest of stalagmites and stalactites. Or was it merely the dancing shadows on the wall?

Frightened, she tried to fight back the terror. She must think, *think*! He was coming. She could hear his footsteps; then they faded. Had he turned another way? If she could only get back through the crack and outside! If she could—

He was there, before her, holding the torch. "Y' better git back the way you come," he said. "If this here torch goes out, we're both in trouble."

She felt around for some kind of weapon, a piece of stone, a broken stalactite . . . anything!

Coolly he wedged the pitch-pine torch into a crack in the wall, then turned toward her. "All right now, filly. The runnin's over. Come here!"

"Tucker?" Bowdrie's voice boomed in the cave. "You wanted me, now I'm here. Drop your gunbelts or start shootin'!"

Bowdrie took a quick step to the left to draw fire away from Lily, and his boot caught on a projecting rock. He tripped and fell, crashing to the rock floor. He heard the girl's quick scream of terror as he thumbed the hammer on the six-gun in his hand.

A lance of fire darted at him. His own crossed it. He heard a gasp and he scrambled to his feet. Across forty feet of torchlit cave the men faced each other.

Was Shad Tucker really hit? Or had his bullet only brought a startled gasp from the outlaw?

Lily shrank against the wall, and Tucker was bringing his gun up. Bowdrie shot from down low and the bullet ripped the gun from Tucker's hand. It fell, rattling among the rocks.

Turning swiftly, Tucker darted into the depths of the cave, running hard. Bowdrie sent a bullet after him, then, as the outlaw was no longer visible, he held his fire. Moving deeper into the shadows.

They heard the running feet, then suddenly a wild,

terror-riven scream. A scream that echoed again and then again in the vaulted room.

Lily Fosdick stared at Bowdrie. "What—?"

"Something happened," he said. He took the torch from the wall and they started through the pillars of stone. Somewhere they heard water falling. Bowdrie stopped abruptly.

The cave floor ended suddenly, and before them gaped a great hole, a huge cistern within the cave. A mouth of blackness that gulped at their feeble light. Picking up a loose stone, he dropped it into the hole. Their eyes stared, listening, waiting. . . .

Then somewhere far, far below there was a splash.

Without a word they walked back to the cave entrance.

Jerry was waiting, gun in hand. He holstered the pistol when he saw them. Briefly Bowdrie explained.

"Got Thomas tied up," Jerry said. "Pa come along an' helped me. Crowley got away. Lit out."

Jerry cleared his throat. "I was goin' to ride with them, Mr. Bowdrie. I really was. Thought I was."

"Point is, you didn't. If you're restless here, ride up north to the XIT. Friends of mine up there, an' they're hirin' for the roundup an' trail drive. That'll be work enough to keep you out of trouble."

"Last night," Lily said, "after you went to the barn to sleep, I made a cake. Icing and all. I haven't even cut into it yet."

Bowdrie's head came up like a hound dog scenting a coon. "Now, that's something I haven't had in more than a year. Shall we ride a little faster?"

Rain on the Mountain Fork

Lew Judd was a frightened man. His hands, white as those of a woman, gathered the cards from the tabletop, and he touched his tongue to dry lips. Overhead the rain was increasing its roar, and within the stuffy warmth of the sod shanty the air was thick with mingled tobacco and wood smoke, overlaid by the odor of wet, steamy clothing, drying wood, and worn leather.

DeVant, Baker, and Stadelmann sat around the table. Peg Roper snored on a bunk against the wall, and Big Ed Colson, the stage driver, straddled a chair and leaned his hairy forearms on its back, watching the play. Judd was sure that Big Ed knew he wore a money belt, but whether the others knew, he could not guess.

"You think the next stage will get through?"

The question was important to Judd. If the stage came soon enough, he might get away, and he might get Nelly away. The stage on which they had come lay hub-deep in mire with a broken axle.

Colson shrugged. "Your guess is as good as mine. This is the worst storm I've seen in this country, an' I've seen a few."

Nelly Craig, Judd's niece, sat beside the fire. It was bad enough to have to escort a young girl through such country without having to stop over in a place like this. As a protector he felt woefully inadequate, yet he kept his face composed, trying to keep the others from realizing his fear.

"We might as well figure on spending the night here," Baker commented. "If the stage does come, it will not get here before morning."

Big Stadelmann turned and stared toward the fire. Judd felt his abdominal muscles tighten, knowing he was staring at Nelly. In the feeble glow of the fire and the kerosene lantern he looked monstrous and brutal, a great bear of a man, his face covered with a stubble of short beard.

DeVant was slender and sallow-faced with malicious yellow eyes, his agile fingers fondling the cards like a lover. All the men were armed, as was the sleeping man on the bunk, and there was a watchfulness about them that warned Judd these were dangerous men.

Colson was armed, but where he would stand, Judd did not know. A postal employee from Minnesota, Judd was new to the country, and although he carried a gun, he was clumsy with it.

The fire sputtered from rain falling down the chimney and in the interval that followed a roll of thunder, they distinctly heard the splash of a horse's hooves on the sloppy trail.

DeVant's head came up sharply, and Stadelmann's hands became still. All were listening. Ed Colson took the pipe from his mouth and turned his head.

"Who in blazes would be riding on a night like this?" Baker demanded. "No man in his right mind would ride in this rain."

They heard the subdued sounds of a man stabling a horse in the sod barn adjoining. Then footsteps splashed and the flames flickered as the door opened to reveal wet boots and above them the lower edge of a slicker as the man stood on the steps closing the slanting door behind him. Judd waited, apprehensive and hopeful at the same time. Baker's hand was in his lap and Judd knew it held a gun. What was he afraid of? What were they all afraid of?

The newcomer came on down the steps, but nothing could be seen of him because of his raincoat collar and his tilted hat brim. The hat was flat-crowned and black, the visible mouth was firm, the jaw strong. His rain-wet chaps were black leather and when he removed the raincoat, he was wearing a fringed buckskin jacket over a gray wool shirt.

He was, they all noted, wearing two guns, tied down.

When he removed his hat to slap the rain from it, they saw a dark, Indian-like face. His eyes swept the room, lingering a bit on Roper, stretched on the bunk. Under his cheekbone there was a deep scar, possibly a bullet wound.

"Who's the owner here?" His tone was casual.

After a moment, when nobody answered, Colson replied. "Place was empty. When the stage broke down, we took shelter. I was drivin' the stage."

Judd looked at him hopefully. "Did you see the other stage on the trail?"

The steady black eyes examined and judged him. "There won't be a stage. A landslide wiped out the trail. Take work to get it back in shape. A lot of work."

DeVant's mind, nimble as his too clever fingers, came up with the logical question. "How did you get here, if the road is closed?"

"I came from the west, but that trail's closed too. I had to come over the mountain above the creek, but I circled to examine the other way out."

Colson took the pipe from his mouth. "You came over the *mountain*? You're lucky to be alive. I wouldn't have thought a goat could make it on a night like this."

"That second slide came while I was up there. Seemed like the whole mountain started to move, but mine's a good horse an' we made it."

Thunder muttered irritably back in the canyons. The rain seemed empowered by the sound and rose to a shattering roar. There was a slow drip of water from near the bunk where Roper slept.

"We're stuck then," DeVant said. "We might as well

make the best of it." He glanced at Nelly, meeting her eyes boldly. "All the comforts of home."

Nelly turned her eyes away and added a stick to the fire. The flames reached for it hungrily, and the stranger moved nearer to the fireplace, aware of her fear. "You were on the stage?" He spoke softly.

There were shaded hollows of tiredness beneath her eyes, which were dark and large. "I am traveling with my uncle, Lew Judd. We are from Illinois."

That would be the slender man in the store-bought suit, a feeble staff on which to lean on such a night, in such a place. She knew he would be of no help and she was frightened.

"Don't be afraid," the stranger said. "It will be all right."

The others heard the murmur of their voices but the words were inaudible. When the stranger looked up, DeVant's catlike eyes were on him. "A man ridin' on a night like this must want to go somewhere mighty bad."

"You could be right." The black eyes held DeVant's and the man felt a distinct chill, which irritated even as it frightened him.

Stadelmann was watching him, eyes suddenly attentive. Peg Roper shifted and muttered on the bunk.

"You were all on the stage?"

Baker's eyes lifted from his cards. His was a narrow, rock-hard face with a clipped mustache on his broad upper lip. "Now you're asking questions?"

The black eyes shifted to Baker and held him an instant before moving on. "That's right. I am asking questions."

The challenge was understood by everyone listening, and for a minute or so there was no sound but the hissing of the raindrops in the fire.

Baker felt something cold and empty in his stomach and he fumbled the cards. The yielding of his eyes enraged him. Yet that voice had rung with the crisp sound of authority.

The stranger turned his attention to Colson. "You were the driver? How many were on that stage?"

"Only Judd, his niece, and DeVant. Stadelmann an' Roper were in the dugout when we got here. Baker came along after."

"Roper was fast asleep when I come in," Stadelmann said. "You got a reason for askin'?"

"Murder's my reason. Murder an' robbery. The killer is in this room. He just can't be anywhere else."

Nelly Craig's face was a blotch of white. Her eyes seemed even larger.

"You're sure he came this way?" Colson asked.

"You know this country. He had no choice. He could have been on the stage or he might have been one of the others."

"You've no description?" Baker asked.

DeVant's eyes lifted from his cards. "Who're you? Askin' all the questions?"

"I'm a Ranger. My name is Bowdrie."

There was a heavy silence in the room. Others here might be wanted men. All at that moment felt guilty, and their resentment was electric in the room.

"You should have kept still about it," Judd said. "Now there will be trouble."

"You can't avoid trouble in this case. One of you here is carryin' money an' the murderer knows it. The murder back yonder was not a planned thing, and the murderer did not get as much as he counted on. It was something he stumbled into."

A stick toppled over into the fire and sent a shower of sparks up the chimney. Nelly moved her wet feet closer to the blaze and Big Ed Colson got out his pipe and stoked it methodically. Peg Roper continued to sleep. Judd sat silent, keeping his palms pressed to the table so their trembling would not be observed. It was Stadelmann he was afraid of, Stadelmann and DeVant, yet he trusted none of them. Not even the Ranger.

"Anybody got any coffee?" Baker suggested. "We might as well wait in comfort."

Bowdrie squatted against the wall. No doubt the killer was the most composed of them all. He alone knew who he was. No betraying clue had been left. Not a clue, only a slight indication of character. Somehow he must lead the murderer to betray himself.

Surprisingly, Nelly seemed revived by the new element introduced by the Ranger's arrival. Attention had been turned from her and other thoughts occupied the minds of the men in the room. More than one might be carrying money, and each would be likely to think himself the intended victim. Any of these men, she reflected, could crush Lew Judd like an insect.

She arose and went to the box Judd had carried into the room and came away with coffee. Colson found a flat stone to be placed among the coals, and retrieved a blackened coffeepot from a shelf. There was darkness back there, a darkness into which they could not see, and when Colson went that way, all eyes followed him. All hands were resting near their guns. Colson returned with the pot and Nelly went about making coffee.

Her quick, homey manner brought relief to the tension, and instead of fear there was a growing levity, as though each had become conscious that he held a seat at a very dramatic show. Underneath it all, however, there was the taut strain of nervous tension. Of them all, Nelly and the stage driver seemed the least affected.

Judd, his own danger alleviated for the moment, opened the case he had carried into the room along with the small box with the coffee, and brought out a mandolin. While they waited for water to boil, he sang, in a fair tenor, "Drill Ye Tarriers," a song sung by Irish railroad builders, and inspired a healthy applause. He then sang "Sweet Betsy from Pike" and "Jenny Jenkins." The listeners came up with requests and the singing continued.

Bowdrie remained quiet against the wall. More than the others possibly could, he realized his own inadequacy. He knew his skill with guns, and that few men were better on a trail, but here he had only the devious path of a man's thinking to follow. He was moving in the dark, only aware that the killer might give himself away. How that was to happen, he did not know. Later, he might ask more questions.

Somehow, tonight, within this shack, the issue would be decided. And it was a narrow place for shooting.

DeVant moved his chair against the wall, a position from which he could survey the room as well as Bowdrie, and from which he could move swiftly to attack, defend, or seek the doubtful shelter of the bunk's corner.

At this moment Peg Roper awakened and sat up, obviously confused by the singing, the smell of coffee, and the crackle of the fire. Swinging his feet to the floor, he caught one spur in the ragged blanket. Disengaging it with care, he sat up, blinking around him, his sleepy little boy's face oddly puzzled under his shock of unruly hair.

"What's comin' off?" Peg asked. "I go to sleep in a morgue and wake up in a party."

"Folks kept dropping in," Baker said. "We've a special guest, a Texas Ranger."

Roper looked uneasy, but said, "Well, he seems a quiet Ranger. Knows how to keep his place."

Bowdrie smiled and put his shoulders against the wall. It was a thick wall and it felt good, about the only security he was likely to enjoy.

Colson found several cups back in the darkness and brought them to the table. He rinsed them with rainwater from the barrel outside the door.

Stadelmann appeared to be dozing and probably was. A man could doze and still catch some of the talk, although nothing important was being said. In fact, everyone seemed to be keeping to casual talk between songs.

Baker changed all that. "How d'you expect to find your man?" he asked Bowdrie. "He ain't just goin' to walk up an' tell you, you know."

"No problem," Bowdrie replied. "Biggest thing in

my favor is that he knows he's guilty. A guilty man is afraid of makin' mistakes, of givin' himself away."

Peg Roper's eyes went to the girl, sitting quietly by the fire, watching the coffee. They stayed on her as she took a cup and poured, taking it first to the Ranger. He thanked her while Roper watched them. Obviously he was curious about her, so strange to such surroundings. Roper rubbed his unshaved chin ruefully. He looked miserable to try to make a play for the girl, but from the looks of it the Ranger had the inside track. Although he did not appear to be doing anything about it. Maybe it was because the Ranger was protection.

Bowdrie tasted the coffee with real appreciation. He was vastly comfortable now, with the cup in his hands, hot coffee in his belly, and that wall behind him. When the side of that mountain started to move back yonder, he had an awful, sinking feeling inside of him and he had been the most scared he'd ever felt. Only the fact that he was riding the roan, a once wild mustang, saved him. The bronc knew what to do, and did it.

Thunder growled in the canyons like a surly dog over a bone, and the fire blazed up, adding light to the room.

Bowdrie let his eyes go closed. One man here was a murderer, but which one? He was a man quick to make decisions, even impulsive. He was utterly ruthless, with a sharp, cold mind and a contempt for human feelings and life. If unmasked he would begin shooting, without warning if possible, and he would not care who got in the way. Yet Bowdrie did know a little about him.

The killer had washed his hands back there at the shack where he murdered the old man. He had washed the blood off the bench and hung up the pan. The old man would not have done that, as he was notoriously untidy.

Bowdrie opened his eyes. "The man I'm looking for," he said, "just stumbled across an old miner an' killed him, prob'ly thinkin' the old man had more'n he did

have. He did this just along the way whilst followin' a
man who he knew had money."

"You'll never get him," Baker said. "What do you
have to go on?"

"Very little," Bowdrie admitted, "but we don't always need a lot. No man can escape the pattern of his
habits. He leaves sign in the minds of people just as he
would on a trail. People observe things and remember
things they often don't recall until questioned or until
the memory is stirred up in conversation."

"That wouldn't stand before a jury," DeVant said.

"No jury will ever get this case," Bowdrie said. "This
gent makes up his mind on the sudden. I'll draw a
pattern of sign to corral him, an' when he realizes I'm
closin' in, he'll go to shootin'. Then he'll die."

"Or you will. Ever think of that, Ranger?"

"Of course. It is an accepted risk in my business, but
Rangers are enlisted because they're fightin' men an'
when they go out they don't go alone. When I go down
that dark trail there'll be a man ahead of me."

"Killer or no killer," Colson said, "we're warm an'
dry in here." He gathered up bits of moss and sticks
fallen from the woodpile and tossed them into the fire.
"Only, if you expect to get your killer, get him before
we get the stage started. Shootin' frets my horses."

Bowdrie went to the fire to refill his cup, and felt
their eyes upon him. Perhaps more than one man here
had reason to fear a Ranger. Mentally he reviewed their
faces, but none rang a responsive chord. His eyes avoided
the fire, knowing the time it takes to adjust back to
shadows after gazing into the flames. Time enough for a
man to die.

He glanced at Roper. "Driftin'?"

"Sort of. I been punchin' cows on the Nueces. Figured I'd head for Mobeetie."

"Good place to stay shut of," Baker commented.
"That black-headed two-gun marshal is poison."

"Not no more," Colson replied. "Killed by a drunken
gambler who pulled a sneak gun on him."

Bowdrie glanced at him. "You boys on the stage lines get all the news."

"West-bound driver told me. Carried one to the other, news travels fast."

Stadelmann glanced at Roper. "If you're through with that bunk, I'd like a try at it."

"She's all yours." Roper moved closer to Bowdrie, studying him. Bowdrie was a man he had heard about.

Bowdrie was not eager to bring the matter to a head now, with the night before them. If he was correct and the killer would elect to shoot it out, this was no place for it. Some innocent person might be killed. Yet soon the light would be blown out and they would try to sleep, and the man with the money would be alone in the dark.

There were detached clues but they pointed in more than one direction, and somehow he must force the issue.

DeVant helped him, without realizing it. "Whoever he is, you've got him trapped. With both roads closed, there's no way out."

"There is, though." Bowdrie was casual. "There's a canyon runs north of here. Looks like a dead end when you ride into it, but she branches out right quick. It would take a rider with nerve and a good horse to make it. That canyon's prob'ly runnin' ten foot deep in water about now."

"That's not for me!" DeVant was emphatic. "I've seen those canyons after a cloudburst."

Ed Colson tamped the tobacco in his pipe and lighted up again. Bowdrie could feel Baker watching him but Big Stadelmann was looking at the girl again.

Lew Judd replaced the mandolin in its case, then moved nearer to Nelly. If there was only some way out! Some means of getting away. He was afraid for Nelly, and for himself. He must have been the man the killer was following, yet how could he have known he was carrying money?

"Need wood," Judd said suddenly. "I'll go after it."

He got up quickly and went out, and Bowdrie felt a twinge of impatience. Didn't the man realize how obvious he was? He must be going outside to cache the money belt. Or was it something else? Why cache the money belt when he would have to recover it again in broad daylight?

Stadelmann got up quickly. "I'll help him. He can't handle enough for all night."

Stadelmann lumbered toward the door and nobody looked at anybody else. As the door opened they all heard the rain and Colson walked over to the fire. Nobody spoke, but all were listening.

Nelly Craig's face was pale as death, and Bowdrie got up, reaching for his slicker. He saw the fear in her eyes and knew she was afraid to be left alone. Bowdrie glanced over at Roper. "If the lady needs anything, see that she gets it, will you?"

Outside the night was black, but for an instant the opening door sent a shaft of light into the rain-streaked darkness. The door closed behind him and Bowdrie stood still.

Somewhere he heard a footstep splash in a pool. He listened and heard no sound but the rain. Where were Judd and Stadelmann?

He turned toward the stable. The stage horses were there as well as his own and the horses ridden by those who had not arrived on the stage. He grinned into the night as he realized what would happen if somebody tried to mount his roan. The horse merely tolerated Bowdrie, but it turned into a fiend if anyone else tried to mount it.

Rain slashed at his face. The stable loomed before him. There was no sound from within, nor could he hear a sound from elsewhere that would lead him to believe anyone was gathering wood. Straining his eyes into the darkness, he suddenly saw starkly revealed in a flash of lightning a huge, looming figure!

Bowdrie sidestepped quickly but his boot came down on something that skidded from under him, and he fell, catching a ringing blow on the skull as he went down. Lights seemed to burst in his brain and he rolled over in the wet, struggling to rise. Another blow stretched him flat and then he rolled over and rain poured over his face. He heard the splash of what sounded like a horse's hoof, then silence.

He tried to rise and the move caused a rush of pain to his head and he blacked out. When he opened his eyes again he had the feeling minutes had passed. He struggled to his feet and stood swaying, his head throbbing with pain.

Who could have hit him? Only his hat and his slipping in the mud had saved him from a cracked skull. He fought back the pain in his head. He had stepped, slipped, and the man had hit him.

A big man . . . *Stadelmann!*

But he could not be certain. It might only have been somebody who looked large in the night, somebody with an enveloping raincoat.

He swung back the door and almost fell down the steps. They stared at him, amazed. Stadelmann, his big face stupid with surprise, DeVant, Baker, Judd . . .

"What happened?" Roper was on his feet. "You're all blood!"

"I got slugged. Somebody slugged me with a chunk of wood."

Nobody moved. Bowdrie's eyes went to Stadelmann. "You were outside."

"So was I." Baker smiled contemptuously. "So were Judd and DeVant, but nobody was out for long."

Nelly came to him with a hot damp cloth. "Here, let me fix your head."

Bowdrie sat as she bathed away the blood, trying to force his thoughts through the foggy jungle of his brain. Were they all working together? Who could he suspect? Peg Roper and Stadelmann had been in the dugout before the stage arrived. Had they planned a holdup? What of Baker? Where had he been? He had apparently come up after the stage arrived, but Bowdrie had seen no tracks on the road he had followed as far as the landslide. No rider had come over the mountain ahead of him.

He was a blockhead! Somewhere here a killer was lurking, ready to kill again. It was very likely that killer who had made an attempt on him a few minutes past, and had he not been fortunate enough to slip in the mud he would be lying out there now, dead as a man could be.

How could he be sure several of these men were not wanted? Or that they were not a gang, working in concert?

Peg Roper acted strangely when he awakened, and Baker had taken pains to let Roper know there was a Ranger present. Had he been afraid Roper would make a break and give them away?

Bowdrie was angry. He did not like being slugged; he liked still less being made a fool. He wanted a trail he could follow, not this feeling around in the dark for an enemy he could not even see. He almost hoped it was Baker, for he had come to dislike the man.

"You know," Judd said, "I thought I heard a horse when I was outside."

Bowdrie's head came up so sharply he winced with pain. "You did," he said. "I heard it too."

"Must be a horse missing, then." DeVant was cool. "What's the matter, Ranger? I thought you fellows had all the answers."

Bowdrie got to his feet again and put on his hat. His head had swelled and the hat fit poorly.

"Want some protection, Ranger?" Baker taunted.

Bowdrie turned at the steps. His black eyes were cold. "Stay here! All of you! I want nobody outside, and if I see anybody, I'll shoot!"

He went out into the night, and it seemed even darker than before. Crossing to the stable, he struck a match and held it high.

The horses turned their heads and rolled their eyes

at him. He counted them, struck a fresh match, and counted again. All were here.

Savagely he threw the match to the floor and rubbed it into the ground with his toe, stepping away quickly so as not to be standing where he had been when he held the match.

He had distinctly heard a horse, but no horses were missing, hence there must be some other rider around. Someone who was not inside the dugout.

He considered that. The shelter they had found was half a sod shanty, half a dugout in the side of a low hill. So far as he could see, there was no place to get in or out but the door. On the other hand, he had not examined the back of the room where Colson had found the coffeepot.

He had heard a horse, but Judd had not been robbed. If the killer was the kind of man Bowdrie believed, he would not leave without robbing Judd.

Bowdrie went back to the dugout. "No horses missing," he said.

"I heard a horse too," Stadelmann said.

"Do you believe in ghosts, Ranger?" Baker smirked.

"Where's Colson?" he asked suddenly.

For the space of three breaths no one replied. Baker looked quickly around, frowning. DeVant got up uneasily. Nelly broke the silence. "Why . . . why, he's gone!"

"When did he go?" Judd asked. "I don't recall when I last saw him."

DeVant looked at Bowdrie. "Colson is a big man, Ranger, but why would he slug you?"

"Don't be foolish!" Baker interrupted angrily. "Why would he want to do that?"

Chick Bowdrie was very still, thinking. "Did any of you talk to him at the last station?"

They looked at each other, then shook their heads. Nobody had. Were there any stops between here and there? No stops.

Colson? Why had he not thought of him? Because he

was, or seemed to be, the stage driver. "If it was him," he muttered, "he had this better planned than I thought."

Baker smiled. "If it was him, Ranger, how did he get out of this dugout without being seen? And where did the horse come from?"

"He didn't go up the steps," Roper said. "I was settin' there all the time."

The coffeepot! Bowdrie stepped around Judd and went into the dark area behind the sideboard. There was a pool of water on the earthen floor from a leak in the roof. He held the lantern high. There was also a wrecked bunk and some old debris. Away from the firelight, the muddy space was damp and cheerless. He looked around; then suddenly they heard an irritated, half-uttered "*Damn!*" The light of the lantern disappeared.

He called back, "There's another room back here. It was where he kept his horse!"

They crowded to look. Beyond the dank, dark space there was a door, not to be seen from the front of the dugout, and the small room beyond it was tight-roofed and dry. There was hay on the floor and a crude manger. Beyond was a door that led outside.

DeVant peered through the peephole in the door. "He must have stood here and watched us at the woodpile. He could see us by lightning flashes, so he knew when to leave."

Judd shoved them aside and plunged past, opening the door to the outside, charging through the dwindling rain to the far side of the woodpile. "It's gone! My money's gone!" he wailed.

White and stricken, he stood over a hole in the woodpile where sticks had been hastily thrown aside. "You hid it here?" Bowdrie asked.

"And he must've stood by that peephole watching me hide it." He stared at Bowdrie. "It was all I had. All! And all she had, too!"

Ed Colson, then, had been here before. Instead of being spur-of-the-moment, this robbery had been part of a carefully conceived plan. Colson had robbed the prospector by taking advantage of an unexpected opportunity, but his appearance as a stage driver was deliberately planned. He must have lurked beside the trail, boarded the stage at some steep grade where it moved slowly, climbed over the back, then knifed or slugged the driver. He must then have taken the reins, gambling that in the darkness no one would know the difference.

The breakdown was undoubtedly deliberate, but the blocked trails and the arrival of Bowdrie had been no part of his plan.

Peg Roper threw wood on the fire and stepped back, watching the flames take hold. DeVant dropped back into his chair and gathered the cards into a stack. Baker smiled, looking around at Bowdrie. "Well, Ranger, now what happens?"

Chick Bowdrie studied a spot on the back of his hand with perplexed eyes. It was a round, red spot slightly fringed on the edges. It was blood. He ignored Baker and shifted his glance to Roper. "You were the first one here?"

"Yeah. The place was cold an' empty. I knew nothing about no back room. I just broke up some kindling an' got a fire goin'. Once she was burnin' pretty good, I put some chunks on the fire an' laid down. I was played out."

"You were next, Stadelmann?"

"Uh-huh. Roper there, he was asleep or pretendin' to be when I come in. I put more wood on the fire an' set down at the table. About that time other folks started arrivin'."

Bowdrie picked up his cup and Nelly filled it from the pot. He sat down in an empty chair with his back to the wall. Right from the start this had been a tough one. He had been searching for a man he had never seen and of whom he had no description. He had found himself among a group of people, any one of whom might be guilty. Now the least likely of them all seemed

to be the man he must find. And that man was gone. Or
was he?

"Roper? The way I understand it, you an' Miss Craig
were in here all the time?" ·

"Uh-huh, only Baker never did go clear out. Just his
head an' shoulders."

DeVant's yellow eyes followed Bowdrie with that
same malicious gleam as his fingers riffled the pasteboards.

Nelly and Roper were near the fire. Judd, his face
drawn and bitter with the loss of his life savings, stood
nearby. Baker and Stadelmann were at the table with
DeVant.

Finishing his coffee, Bowdrie took off his wet slicker
and hung it on a nail. Then he dried his hands with
infinite care, his dark Apache features inscrutable as he
carefully thought out every move. What he would now
attempt to do was fraught with danger.

He turned suddenly. "Stadelmann! Baker! Get up,
will you, please?"

Puzzled, they got to their feet. Baker was on the
verge of a sarcastic comment when Bowdrie said, "Now,
if you will go into the back room and take the body of
Ed Colson down from the rafters."

"*What?*" Stadelmann exclaimed.

Judd was staring, jaw hanging.

"Don't bring the body in here, just take it down."

DeVant was watching him, alert and curious. Lew
Judd passed a shaking hand over his chin. "You . . .
you mean he's *dead?*"

"Murdered and robbed after he had robbed you,
Judd, by the only man who could have done it."

"What? What do you mean?" Baker demanded.

"Why, DeVant did it," Bowdrie said, and the two
guns thundered at once.

Bowdrie stood still, his .44 Colt balanced easy in his
hand, while DeVant sat perfectly still, a round hole
over his right eye. Slowly he started to rise, then toppled across the table. Nelly Craig screamed.

White-faced, Baker stared from one to the other,

unable to grasp what had happened. Bowdrie stepped over to the dead man, and unfastening his shirt, removed Lew Judd's money belt and passed it to him.

Judd grasped it eagerly. "Thank God!" His voice trembled. "I slaved half my life for that!"

Peg Roper stared at Bowdrie, and exclaimed, "Did you see him throw that gun? DeVant had his in his lap with his hand on it, an' Bowdrie beat him!"

"How could you know?" Baker asked. "How could you possibly know?"

Bowdrie fed a cartridge into his pistol and holstered it. "I should have known from the beginning. Ed Colson killed that prospector, and he probably killed the stage driver.

"Somehow, DeVant got wise. Maybe he actually heard or saw something back there on the grade. Maybe he was following Judd himself. ·

"Judd an' Stadelmann went after wood and I followed them. Colson had been to the back of the dugout before, and he went there again. He slipped out, tried to kill me, and robbed Judd's cache almost as soon as Judd hid it. He thought he pulled it off, but DeVant had seen him go.

"Probably DeVant knew who to watch. Naturally, Roper and Nelly were looking toward the dugout door where Baker had gone. DeVant was a quiet-moving man, anyway, who knew from card-cheating the value of doing things by misdirection. He got back there, knifed Colson when he came back with the money, and shoved the body across the rafters. Then he just quietly came back into the room. I doubt if the whole operation took him more than two or three minutes.

"Remember, nobody knew there was another room then. All he would seem to have done was to get up and move around."

"What about Colson's horse?"

"Turned it loose with a slap on the rump. DeVant had no reason to be suspected. He planned to ride out on the stage with the rest of you. It was cold, unadulterated gall, but he might have gotten away with it. Only when I was in that back room a drop of blood hit my hand.

"Figure it out. Who was missing? Only Colson. Where could that drop have come from except overhead? It had to be those low rafters. Who had the opportunity? DeVant.

"Baker said DeVant was outside, but he wasn't. That indicated to me that DeVant was moving around. Probably Baker *thought* he had gone out because he was not in sight, but he wasn't paying that much attention."

"I wasn't," Baker said. "I was expecting gunfire out there."

Nobody said anything for several minutes; then Lew Judd sat down and looked at his niece, smiling. "We're going to make it now, honey," he said.

Stadelmann crossed to the bunk and stretched out on the hard boards. He was soon asleep. Roper hunkered down near the fire.

"It is almost morning," Baker said. "Maybe the stage will get through."

"I hope so," Judd said sincerely.

Chick Bowdrie said nothing at all. He was sitting against the wall, almost asleep.

HISTORICAL NOTE:

ESPANTOSA LAKE

Long ago it was believed that the lake and its shores were haunted, and over the years it became a place of legend, ghostly sightings, and mysterious disappearances. On the Upper Presidio Road, which lead from Coahuila in Mexico to the Spanish settlements of Texas, it was in the beginning a favored stopping place. Trains carrying supplies to the missions stopped here, and outlaws lived in the brush country around it. Indians camped here, but rarely were their camps on the lake shore itself. They preferred to camp away from the water.

It has been said that a wagon train loaded with silver and gold camped beside the lake one night and in the morning was gone. Supposedly the ground beneath it sank suddenly, swallowing up all the wagons, stock, and people of the train. In any event, none of them were ever seen again.

The shores of Lake Espantosa were said to be the place where the lost colonists of Dolores disappeared. An attempt was made by a party of English people to establish a colony. After much hardship and struggle they gave up the effort and were headed for the Gulf Coast and a ship home to England. They camped on the shores of Espantosa and vanished, wiped out, some say, by Comanches.

Strange Pursuit

Years had brought no tolerance to Bryan Moseley. Sun, wind, and the dryness of a sandy sea had brought copper to his skin and drawn fine lines around his pale blue eyes. The far lands had touched him with their silence, and the ways of men as well as the ways he had chosen brought lines of cruelty to his mouth and had sunk thoughts of cruelty deep into the convolutions of his brain, so deeply they shone forth in the flat light of his eyes.

"No, I don't know where he is. If I did know, I wouldn't tell you. Don't tell me I'm going to hang. I heard the judge when he said it. Don't tell me it'll relieve my soul because whatever burden my soul carries, it will carry to the end. I lived my life and I'm no welsher."

Chick Bowdrie sat astride the chair, his arms resting on the back, his black hat on the back of his head. He found himself liking this mean old man who would cheerfully shoot him down if he had a chance to escape.

"Your soul is your problem, but Charlie Venk is mine. I've got to find him."

"You won't find him settin' where you are."

"Known him long?"

"You Rangers know everything, so you should know that, too." The old outlaw's eyes flared. "Not that I've any use for him. He never trusted me an' I never trusted him. I will say this. He is good with a gun. He is as good as any of them. He was even better'n me. If he hadn't been I'd have killed him."

"Or was it because you needed him? You were gettin' old, Mose."

The old man chuckled without humor. "Sure, I could use him, all right. Trouble was, he used me."

"How was that?" Bowdrie took out a sack of tobacco and papers and tossed them to the prisoner. "I figured you for the smartest of them all."

"Just what I figured." Mose took up the tobacco and began to build a smoke. "Don't think you're gettin' around me, I just feel like talkin'. Maybe it is time they hung me. I *am* gettin' old."

He sifted tobacco into the paper. "We had that bank down in Kelsey lined up. I done the linin'. Never did trust nobody to do that. The others always overlooked something. On'y thing I overlooked was Charlie Venk.

"You seen him? He's a big, fine-lookin' young man. Strong-made, but quick. I seen plenty of 'em come an' go in my time. Seen the James boys an' the Youngers. Cole, he was the best of that lot. Jesse, he had a streak of meanness in him, like the time he shot that schoolboy with his arms full of books. No need for it.

"Charlie reminded me of Cole. Big man, like Cole, an' good-lookin'. I never trust them kind. Always figure they're better'n anybody else. 'Cept maybe Cole. He never did.

"We got that bank job lined up. There was four of us in it. Charlie, Rollie Burns, Jim Sloan, an' me, of course. Burns an' Sloan, they were bad. Mean men, if you know what I mean, and they couldn't be trusted. Not that it mattered, because I never trusted anybody myself. An' nobody ever trusted me.

"Ever see Charlie sling a gun? I've heard you're fast, Bowdrie, but if you ever tangle with Charlie you'll go down. Not only is he fast but he can lay 'em right where he wants 'em, no matter how rough it gets.

"He was slick on a trail, too, but if you've already trailed him across three states, you know that. He was a first-rate horse thief. Given time, I'll tell you about that.

"Anyway, about noon we come down this street into town. No nice town like this'n. She was a dusty, miserable place with six saloons, two general stores, a bank, and a few odds and ends of places. We come in about noon, like I say. Sloan, he was holdin' the horses, so the rest of us got down an' went in.

"There was a woman an' two men in that bank. Two customers an' the teller. Rollie, he put his gun on the woman an' the man customer an' backed them into a corner, faced against the wall. At least, the man was. Rollie, he didn't pay much mind to the woman.

"Charlie, he pushed the teller over alongside of them an' vaulted the rail to start scoopin' money into a sack.

"Out front Sloan leans over to look into the bank an' he says, 'Watch it! The town's wakin' up fast!'

"Charlie, he was a smooth worker with no lost motion and he had cleaned up more cash than I had. We started for the door an' the teller, he takes a dive for his desk. Maybe he had a gun back there. Rollie backs his hammer to shoot an' Charlie says, 'Hold it, you fool!' An' he slaps the teller with his gun barrel an' the teller hit the floor cold as a wedge.

"Then we hit the leather and shot our way out of town. We rode like the devil for those first six miles, knowin' there would be a posse. Then we reached the grove where more horses were waitin'. It taken us on'y a moment to switch saddles. We rode out at a canter an' held it, knowin' the posse would almost kill their horses gettin' to that grove.

"We got away. Ten miles further we switched horses for the third and last time. By then the posse was out of the runnin' and we doubled back in the hills, headed for our hangout. Rollie was ridin' a grouch an' Charlie, he was singin'. Nice voice, he had.

"Suddenly Rollie says, his voice kind of funny, 'Nobody

calls me a fool!' We all look around an' he had the drop on Charlie. Had the gun right on him. Well, what d'you expect? Me an' Sloan, we just backed off. Whoever won, it was more money for the rest of us, an' Charlie had always figured he was pretty salty. He was, too. Right then we found out how salty.

" 'Aim to kill me, Rollie?'

" 'What d'you expect? I had that durned teller dead to rights.'

" 'Sure you did,' Charlie said, easy-like. 'Sure you did. But maybe that teller had a wife and kids. If you've got no thought for them, think of this. Nobody back there is dead. All that's gone is the bank's money. Nobody will run us very far for that, but if we killed a family man they'd never quit.' "

"He was right," Bowdrie said.

" 'You ain't talkin' yourself out o' this!' Rollie says. 'I aim to—'

"Charlie Venk shot him right between the eyes. That's right! Got him to talkin' an' off guard, then drew an' fired so fast we scarcely knowed what happened. Rollie, he slid from the saddle an' Charlie never looked at him. He just looked at us. He had that gun in his hand an' was smilin' a little. 'I wasn't askin' for trouble,' he said. 'You boys want to take it up?'

" 'Hell no! Rollie always had a grouch on,' Sloan says. 'Leave him lay.'

"We camped that night at a good place Charlie knew. Three ways out, good water, grass an' cover. We ate good that night. Charlie, he was a good cook when he wanted to be, an' he really laid it on. Like a dumb fool, I ate it up an' so did Sloan. After all, none of us had et a good meal in a week. We et it up an' then Charlie outs with a bottle an' we had a few drinks. Charlie was a talker, an' he was yarnin' away that night in a low, kind of dronin' voice. An' we'd come a hard ride that day. Before we knew it, we were dozin'.

"Of a sudden I come awake an' it was broad daylight! Yessir, I'd fallen asleep right where I lay, boots an' all!

What made me maddest of all was that I'd figured on gettin' up whilst the others were asleep an' skippin' with the cash.

"There was Sloan, still fast asleep. An' Charlie? You guessed it. Charlie was gone.

"He had hightailed. No, he didn't take our money but he did take Rollie's share, but that was half of it. Oh, yeah! He dipped into our share for a dollar each an' left a note sayin' it was for the extra grub an' the whiskey. Why, that—!"

Bowdrie chuckled. "You never saw him again?"

"Not hide nor hair." Mose got to his feet. "You catch up with him, you watch it. Charlie's got him some tricks. Slips out of cuffs, ropes, anything tied to his wrists. Mighty supple, he is. I seen him do it.

"Good at imitatin', too. He can listen to a man talk, then imitate him so's his own wife wouldn't know the difference."

One hundred and four miles north, the cowtown of Chollo gathered memories in the sun. Along the boardwalk a half-dozen idlers avoided work by sitting in the shade. Chick Bowdrie's hammerhead roan sloped along the street like a hungry hound looking for a bone.

Outside the livery stable a man kept his stomach on his knees by using a rope for a belt. When Bowdrie swung to the ground the flesh around what seemed to be one of the man's chins quivered and a voice issued, a high, thin voice.

"Hay inside, oats in the bin, water at the trough. He'p yourself an' it's two bits the night. You stayin' long?"

"Just passin' through." Bowdrie shoved his hat back on his head, a characteristic gesture, and watched the roan. Bowdrie lived with the roan the way Pete Kitchen had lived with Apaches. Safe as long as he watched them.

"Any strangers around?"

"Rarely is. Rarely."

"Ever hear of Charlie Venk?"

"Nope."

"Big gent, nice-lookin', an' prob'ly ridin' a black horse. Good with his gun."

Both eyes were wide open now, and the fat man peered at him with genuine interest. "We never knowed his name. Never saw him use a gun, but we know him. He's the gent that hung our sheriff."

"Hung your *what*?"

"Sheriff. Ed Lightsen." A fat middle finger pointed. "Hung him to that big limb on the cottonwood yonder."

"He hung the *sheriff*?"

A chuckle issued from the rolls of fat. "Uh-huh. He surely did! Best joke aroun' here in a year. The sheriff, he was aimin' to hang this gent, an' he got hung hisself. Funny part of it was, it was the sheriff's own rope."

The fat man leaned forward. There were rolls of fat on the back of his neck and shoulders.

"This gent you speak of. Venk, his name was? He come in here about an hour before sunset ridin' a wore-out bronc. He was carrying some mighty heavy saddlebags an' he was a big man himself, an' that bronc had been runnin'.

"Nobody has any extry horses in this town. All out on roundups. Stingy with 'em, anyway. This gent, he tried to buy one, had no luck a-tall, but he hung around. Split a quart with the boys over at the saloon. Sang 'em some songs an' yarned with 'em. Come sundown, he walked out of there an' stole the sheriff's sorrel.

"That's right, the sheriff's sorrel. Now, the sheriff had been makin' his brag that nobody but him could ride that horse. This here Venk, as you call him, he got astride an' he stayed astride for just one mile. Then he came head-on into ten of those hard-case riders of Fairly's. They recognized the horse and threw down on him before he even realized he was in trouble. They brought him back into town.

"Now, the sheriff was mighty sore. I don't know whether it was for stealin' the horse or because this

here Venk actually rode him. 'You can put him in jail,'
Webb Fairly says, but the sheriff was havin' none of it.
'Jail? For a horse thief? We'll hang him!'

"There was argyment, but not much. It looked to be
a quiet time in town, so the boys figured a hangin'
would liven things up a mite. Then this here Venk
comes up with his own argyment.

" 'Well, boys, you got me. I guess I've come to the
end of my trail, but I'll be damned if I go out with
money in my pocket. Nor should a man be hung with a
dry throat. I don't favor that, an' I reckon you boys
don't.

" 'Actually, I feel sorry for you. Here you come to
town for fun, now you've got to hang me. So let's go
over to the saloon an' drink up my money.' "

The fat man hitched up that rope belt, which did no
good, and shrugged. "Well, now. Who's to argy agin
that? We all lit a shuck over to Bob's, an' this horse
thief showed hisself a true-blue man. He had 'em set
out eight bottles. That's right, *eight*!

"Webb Fairly, he said, 'Stranger, if there was ary
thing to do in town tonight, we'd not hang you! But you
know how it is?'

"Those eight bottles went quick, and that stranger
bought four more. By that time ever'body was palooted,
but nobody had forgot the hangin'. This here was a
story to tell their grandchildren! It was almighty dark,
but this Venk, as you say his name was, he told us,
'Boys,' he says, 'when I was a youngster I played under
cottonwood trees. I noticed a big ol' cottonwood down
the street by the blacksmith shop, an' if you'd hang me
from that tree I'd be almighty proud!'

"Why not? We agreed. It isn't ever' day a man gits
hung, an' it ain't ever' day we hang a gent who stages
his own wake, sort of.

"It was little enough to do. Now, that there cottonwood was in the darkest place in town and we rode over
there. We felt this feller was gettin' mighty sad, as he

sort of choked up an' we heard what we figured was sobbin'.

"Nobody likes to hear a growed man cry, least of all a dead-game sport like this stranger, so we turned our faces away, slung a rope over the branch, and the sheriff—at least we figured it was the sheriff—he puts the noose over this man's head an' says, 'Let 'er go, boys!' an' the sorrel jumped out from under him and that gent was hangin' right where he wanted it. We watched him kick a mite an' then the sheriff says, 'Drinks are on me, boys, an' the last one into the saloon's a greenhorn!'

"We taken out on the run for the saloon and it was not until two drinks later we realized the sheriff wasn't with us.

"Nobody paid it much mind, 'cept one o' the boys did speak up an' say, 'You know? He must take to hangin', because that's the first time the sheriff ever bought anybody a drink!'

"Come daylight, those of us who could walk started for home, an' when we seen that gent hangin', we went over for a last look, an' what d'you think? We'd hung the sheriff!"

The fat man slapped his thigh and chuckled. "Funniest thing happened around here in years! That gent sure had him a sense of humor! Somehow he'd got those ropes off his wrists an' he must have slugged an' gagged the sheriff. Then he slipped that noose over . . .

"But I'd have sworn that was the sheriff! I heard him plain! He—"

"Charlie Venk is a good mimic," Bowdrie commented. "Did you try to trail him?"

"What for? We figured it was a good joke on the sheriff, an' he wasn't much account, anyway."

There was a trail when Bowdrie left town, a good clean trail, as the sorrel had a nice stride. Bowdrie followed the trail into an area of small rolling hills, across slabs of rock that left but indistinct white scars to mark Venk's passing, and when Bowdrie rode up to the next water hole there was a message scratched in the mud.

Whoever's trailin' me better light a shuck. I ain't foolin'.

Bowdrie glanced at it, then drank and filled his canteen and led the roan to drink. As the horse drank, Bowdrie's eyes kept moving, and when he was again in the saddle he continued his searching of the hills. His dark features were somber, for he had no illusions about the man he trailed. Charlie Venk watched his back trail, and Venk would be either seeing him now or at some time within the next few minutes. From here on it would be tough, and the advantage lay with Venk in that he knew where he was going and could choose the ground. If he wanted a battle, he could also choose the place.

Four years now Bowdrie had been riding with the Rangers, and if they wanted a man, they got him. If not now, later, but get him they would.

The odds were all against the criminal, for the law had time, and the law was tireless. An outlaw might scoff and claim that he was "smarter than any dumb Ranger." Even that was doubtful, but was he smarter than fifty Rangers? And the thousands of citizens who had eyes in their heads and could remember?

Very few things that people do remain unnoticed by somebody. All the law has to do is find that somebody who saw or heard something. Not always easy, but always possible.

Bowdrie rode on into the dancing heat waves where the dust devils did their queer, dervishlike dances out upon the white bottoms where no water was. Blue lakes appeared and vanished. Again and again he lost the trail. Again and again he found it.

He followed the man on the sheriff's sorrel where the only trace was left by the wind, and he followed him where the wind died and curled itself in sleep among the dead hills or against the hot flat faces of the cliffs. By desert, ridge, and mountain, by alkali sink and timberline, by deep green forest and bald hill, through lands where the ghosts of long-dead Apaches rode, and to the trails where the stages followed their rutted routes.

He ate where Venk had eaten, slept where he had slept, and came to know his little ways and how he thought and acted. He drank with men who had drunk with Venk, and four times he found places where Venk had circled back to get a look at the strange dark rider who followed him. Then the trail disappeared. It ended at the edge of an alkali lake and there was nothing . . . not a track, not a wisp, simply nothing at all.

Yet the trail of a man is not left on sand alone or on the broken twigs or the scars upon rock. The trail of a man is worked into the way he thinks and in what he wants, so the silent Ranger rode on, his mind reaching out ahead of his horse. His thoughts crossed ridges and searched out in memory of towns he knew and of talk among Rangers as to places and possibilities, and one Saturday afternoon Bowdrie rode into a quiet little cowtown.

He was, he believed, four days behind the sheriff's sorrel, but he had noticed the stride was shorter. Occasionally the sorrel stopped; there had been places where it was almost too tired to graze. The sorrel was going to have to stop or fall dead in its tracks. The roan was unchanged. It was just as tireless and just as mean as ever.

When Bowdrie rode into town, almost the first thing he saw was the sorrel, standing head hanging, in a corral. When he rode closer, he could see the horse had been curried, cared for. He rode his own horse to a livery stable, led it to a stall, fed, watered, and curried it. Few western horses were used to being curried. The roan was, and it liked it, but had no intention of letting its rider know. Twice the roan tried to kick, and once it reached around to nip the Ranger. Bowdrie skillfully avoided the nip with a skill born of long experience, cuffed the roan lightly on the nose, and walked to a bench.

He sat down on the bench, and one at a time, keeping one always loaded and ready for use, he cleaned his guns.

There were nine saloons in town, and the usual assortment of subsidiary structures. The town was like other such towns in other such places. The same horses dozed at the hitching rails, the same dogs slept in the dust, and their tails slapped the dust or the gray boards as he approached with the pleasant acknowledgment that all was friendly in this sunny, dusty world and all they wanted was to be left alone.

Chick Bowdrie pushed through the bat-wing doors and walked to the bar. He accepted the rye whiskey pushed toward him and downed a glass, then filled it again. His eyes kept to the bar, then lifted to the mirror behind it. His mind spelled out the faces in the room. The man he wanted was not present, but he had not expected him to be.

An aging cowhand in faded blue denim with a tobacco tag hanging from his breast-pocket, his face seamed with years, weather, kindness, and irony. The town drunk; his face was a mirror for lost illusions, his eyes hungry with hope, his boots worn, and the old hands trembling. The solid, square-built rancher with new heels on his boots and an air of belligerent prosperity and affluence. The bartender, slightly bald back of the plastered black hair above a smooth, ageless face and brow. The wise, cold eyes and the deft, active hands.

They were types, men without names, faces from a page of life he had turned many times, and faces he had often seen, like the husky young cowboy at the end of the bar who had a split lip and a welt on his cheekbone.

A movement stirred beside him and Bowdrie's muscles relaxed like those of a cat, relaxed to a poised alertness that preceded movement.

In the mirror he saw it was the drunk. Sober now, but hopeful.

"Howdy, stranger." He looked at Bowdrie in the mirror. "I could use a dollar."

Bowdrie's expression did not change. "If I gave you a dollar, how do I know you wouldn't spend it for food?"

For a moment the drunk simply blinked. Then he drew himself up and with great dignity replied, "Sir, I assure you that no such idea ever crossed my mind."

Bowdrie's eyes wrinkled at the corners. "I'm in a good mood. I'll buy you a drink, and then you can show me where the best restaurant is and we'll eat. Both of us. After that, I'll buy you another drink."

They had their drink. "A quiet town," Bowdrie suggested. "A good place to sleep."

"You should have seen it last night. See that gent with the split lip? He got himself into an argument with a big stranger. He had two partners to help, but this stranger, he whipped all three."

"Is he still around?"

"Seemed like he was in a hurry when he came into town, but that was before he saw Lucy Taylor."

"What was the argument about?"

"Whether Tuscaloosa was in Alabama or Arkansas." The drunk looked regretfully at his empty glass, but Bowdrie was starting for the door. He was tired of fixing his own grub and he was a lousy cook, anyway. The drunk followed him, talking. "This here stranger said it was in Arkansas. One word led to another, and they started to slug it out. Mister, that stranger was hell on a bicycle! He whipped the three of them."

"Who is this Lucy Taylor you mentioned?"

"Purtiest gal in these parts. Or any parts, for that matter. Lives yonder by the creek where you see all those cherry blossoms. That big stranger, he seen her an' fell like a ton of bricks, and, mister, if that gent can court like he can fight, he's top man around here now, although Lucy is mighty hard to get."

"Who did he fight with? Local men?"

"You know, I been thinking about that. All three of those gents were courting Lucy. He simply wiped out all the competition at one stroke."

Chick smiled. "Want to know something? That man who did the fighting was born in Alabama. In Tuscaloosa."

"But he claimed it was Arkansas!"

"Know any better way of startin' a fight than by insistin' a man is dead wrong when he *knows* he's right?"

"He started that fight a-purpose?"

"They were courtin' this Lucy you speak of. He fell for Lucy. If they get beat up, they can't go callin' for days. So how does that brand read?"

Among the cherry trees was a house built of native stone, vine-clad and lovely. Nearby was a stream shaded by willows and cottonwoods, and one big cottonwood loomed over the back porch of the house and the yard before it. A girl in a clean, starched gingham dress was hanging clothes on the line.

Her hair was strawberry blond, over a very cute nose a few freckles were scattered, and when she stood on tiptoe to pin clothes on the line, Bowdrie noticed she had very pretty legs.

Removing his hat after a careful glance around, he said, "Good mornin', ma'am."

She turned quickly, with three clothespins in her mouth. He laughed and she hastily removed the clothespins. Then she laughed too. She *was* pretty!

"You surprised me. Are you looking for Dad?"

"Who would look for your father when you're here?"

"Wait until I get these things hung out to dry and I'll get you some coffee. Are you the one who is looking for Charlie Venk?"

Surprised, he said, "Why, yes. Were you expectin' somebody?"

"He told me you'd be along. Said to treat you real nice. He said you'd had a long, hard ride and were probably all worn out. He said age was catching up with you, and long rides were hard on you."

"I'm no older than he is," Bowdrie protested. "Is he still around?"

She hung the last garment. "Come inside. The coffee should be ready by now." She led the way, speaking over her shoulder. "You're here two days earlier than Charlie expected."

"Known him long?"

"Only one day. It seems like I've known him forever." She blushed a little. "He's very handsome." She filled the cup. "And he's not like the boys around here."

"No, I reckon he ain't," Bowdrie said dryly.

"He said you were probably a Texas Ranger."

"I reckon he was right, ma'am." Bowdrie glanced at the rows of books on the shelves behind her. Many of the titles were foreign, some French, some German. "You folks keep a lot of books. I never had a chance to get much schoolin'."

"My father taught me. He was a college man. He is a lawyer."

They talked idly and drank coffee. Finally she went to the sideboard and cut a piece of pie for him. He ate it with appreciation.

"You sure can cook, bake, or whatever," he said. "No wonder Charlie was taken with you. Although," he added, "I don't think it was just the cookin'." He paused. "A right curious kind of man, that Charlie Venk."

"I think he's a fine man!" she insisted indignantly. "He said you began chasing him because of a horse he borrowed. Why didn't you give him time to explain?"

Bowdrie looked as meek as he could and said nothing.

"I think it's a shame! You turn a nice young man like that into a criminal! And over nothing!"

Chick Bowdrie looked regretfully into his empty cup. "Trouble was," he replied mildly, "there was a man settin' on that horse he wanted to borrow."

"On it?" She was puzzled.

"Yes, ma'am. Charlie was in a sort of hurry to leave

because of some other problems he had, and he needed a horse right bad and this gent objected."

"Well?"

"Charlie shot him out of the saddle."

"I don't believe it!"

"No, ma'am. I don't reckon you do. If a man is young and nice-lookin' and is somebody you know, you just don't believe those things about him, but the State of Texas believes it, ma'am, an' that's why I'm here."

He got up from the table just as a tall older man came into the room. He nodded at Bowdrie.

"Good evening, sir."

The older man turned to Lucy and spoke quickly in French. She glanced at Bowdrie, who was staring at the books on the shelf. He took one down that was printed in English. It was a copy of Plutarch's *Lives of Illustrious Men*. The girl's father noticed it.

"You must have a gift for choosing the best. Are you familiar with this book?"

"Carried it in my saddlebags for two years. Gent gave me a copy when I was fourteen. Took me a while to read it." He glanced at the older man. "I never got much schoolin'. Learned to read some, an' cipher. But Plutarch, I grew up with that book. Used to set by the campfire an' study over it, tryin' to make out what was meant. I finally got around to it."

He glanced from the man to Lucy. "This time it just sort of fell open to the part about Alcibiades. Now, there was a nice-seeming young fellow who came from a good family, had good education, just about everything. But he turned out to be a traitor and worse.

"Just goes to show you. A man may be good in some respects, no good in others."

Lucy Taylor flashed her eyes at him, then glanced away. Chick Bowdrie picked up his hat and turned to go. "Reckon I better be gettin' on. I don't want Charlie to get too much lead on me."

"*What?*" Lucy turned swiftly. "What do you mean?"

Bowdrie's slow smile gathered around the corners of

his eyes and then he spoke in French. "I heard what your father said, and your reply, so I know that Charlie saw me and has gone. I know he was hidden not far away when I arrived. And you knew it."

"You speak French! You told me you had not been to school!"

"Ma'am, I grew up down Castroville way, around there an' D'Hanis. Now, when I was a youngster most folks around there spoke both French and German. I learned to speak those languages as soon as I did English.

"You should take no more for granted from an officer of the law than from a horse thief. Both parties might conceal more than they tell."

Charlie Venk had ridden west, then north. Bowdrie knew a showdown was approaching and he was almost sorry. Trailing Venk had been a rare experience. In a time when many men lived by the gun, some of them were men of education and background. John Ringo and Elza Lay, for example, were men of considerable reputation. Charlie Venk was another, yet whatever else he was, he was a killer and a thief.

All that day and much of the next he followed Venk through a maze of tracks. He lost the trail, then found it again. It led across bare hillsides where Venk could proceed swiftly but Bowdrie, for fear of an ambush, must move slowly. He had to ride with extreme care for he was sure that Venk had made up his mind. He was through running.

Venk knew every trick, and he tried them all. Then Bowdrie came on a wagon loaded with household goods. The driver and a woman sat on the wagon seat; a small child peered between their shoulders.

"Hi!" The driver drew up. "You're ridin' the wrong way! Apaches raidin'! Killed a couple of prospectors night before last and burned some folks out! Better head back t'other way!"

Bowdrie smiled. "Thanks. Have you seen a big man?

Ridin' a sorrel horse? Nice-lookin' man, headed the same way I am?"

"Sure did! He he'ped me fix a busted wheel. Bought some ca'tridges from me. You a friend o' his'n?"

"You might put it that way."

"He said he had a friend foller'n him an' he aimed to take that friend right through the middle of Apache country. Said he'd take him right back to Texas if he had the nerve to foller!"

Chick Bowdrie looked south and west. "I imagine he expected you'd tell me that. See you."

He continued north, but now he rode with greater caution, avoiding skylines and studying country before trusting himself to cross open places. Off to the northwest there was a thin column of smoke. It was not a signal. Something was burning.

Bowdrie turned the roan toward it.

Venk, Bowdrie reflected, was a strange combination. He had rustled cattle, stolen horses, robbed banks, and had killed several men, most of them in gun battles. As to the killing that started Bowdrie on his trail when he shot the man off the horse, all the evidence was not in. There might be more to it than the cold-blooded killing it seemed to be.

He was shrewd and intelligent. He could be friendly, and he could be dangerous. He could smile right into your eyes and shoot you dead in your tracks. Whatever else he was, to ride into Apache country meant he had to be either a very brave man or a fool. Or both.

For Bowdrie to follow him was equally foolish. Yet Charlie thought he was playing his ace in taking the risk. Desperate the man might be, but he also knew something about Chick Bowdrie by now.

He could not shake Bowdrie from his trail. Venk had tried every ruse used in wild country. This would be his last attempt.

They were now in northern Arizona. It was the home country of the Mogollon and White Mountain Apache, a rough, broken country of mountains, cliffs, and canyons.

Not many miles from here was a pine forest of considerable extent. Bowdrie would have to think and move carefully, for the Apaches were more to be feared than Venk.

Venk was no fool, and in saying he was returning to Texas, he might do just that. He might also weave a trail through raiding Apache bands, then circle back to pay another visit to Lucy Taylor. Lingering in this country was a foolhardy matter, but better to linger than to act and blunder.

Ten miles ahead of Bowdrie was Charlie Venk. Always before he had been able to talk or laugh himself out of a situation or his skills had been great enough to elude pursuit. He now knew the identity of his pursuer, and he could not have missed knowing something about Bowdrie.

He could find no way of eluding his pursuer, and good with a gun as he was, he knew that in any gun battle many things might happen, and Bowdrie would not die easily. He might kill Bowdrie, but he might also be killed. And Charlie Venk loved life.

He was fresh out of tricks. Several times he believed he had lost the Ranger, but always Bowdrie worked out the trail and kept coming. It was getting on Venk's nerves. He no longer felt like laughing. Twice lately he had awakened in a cold sweat, and he found himself looking over his shoulder constantly. Once he even shot into a shadow. He had not had a good night's sleep in weeks.

Now he was riding into Apache country. There was no mercy in Charlie Venk. He was a good fellow as long as it cost him nothing. Could he have killed Bowdrie without danger to himself, he would have done it.

Nowhere in sight was there movement. Hot sun lay down the valley, but it was cool in the shade and the trail was visible for miles. Cicadas sang in the brush, and somewhere not far off a magpie fussed and worried over something. Charlie Venk needed rest, and this was as good a place as he was apt to find. He would just—

A brown arm slipped from behind and across his throat. Hands seized his arms and he was thrown to the ground. Other Apaches moved in, and he was a prisoner. His arms were bound, his guns taken away.

Blankly he stared into the cruel dark faces around him. He could talk, but his words would fall on unheeding ears. He could laugh, but they would not comprehend. His guns were gone, his muscles bound, his gift of tongue useless.

Charlie Venk stared into the sunlit afternoon realizing the heart-wrenching truth that he was through. He, the handsome, the strong, the ruthless, the untouchable. He who had ridden wild and free was trapped.

He was too wise in the ways of his country not to know what awaited him. Fiendish torture, burning, shot full of arrows or staked to an anthill.

Chick Bowdrie found the spot where the capture took place, not two hours after Venk was taken. He found the stubs of three cigarettes, a confusion of tracks, mingled moccasins and boots. He found the trail that led away, several unshod horses and one shod. There was no blood on the ground. No stripped and mutilated body. Charlie Venk had been taken alive.

It was after nightfall when he found the Apache camp. His horse was tied in a thicket a half-mile away, and Bowdrie had changed to the moccasins he carried in his saddlebags. He was among the rocks overlooking the Apache camp.

Below him a fire blazed and he could see Venk tied to a tree whose top had been lopped off. As Chick watched, an Apache leaped up and rushed at Venk, striking him with a burning stick. Another followed, then another. This was preliminary; the really rough stuff was still to come. There were at least twenty Apaches down there, some of them women and children.

Bowdrie inched forward, measuring the risk against

the possibilities. Coolly he lifted his Winchester. His mouth was dry, his stomach hollow with fear. Within seconds he would be in an all-out fight with the deadliest fighters known to warfare.

His greatest asset aside from his marksmanship was surprise. What he must do must be done within less than a minute.

He fired three times as fast as he could lever the shots. The range was point-blank. The first bullet was for a huge warrior who had jumped up and grabbed a stub of blazing wood and started for Venk. The bullet caught the Indian in mid-stride.

Bowdrie swung his rifle and another Apache dropped, a third staggered, then vanished into the darkness.

Instantly he was on his feet. If he was to free Venk, it must be done now! Once the panic inspired by the sudden attack was over, he would have no chance at all.

A move in the shadows warned him, and he fired. Venk was fighting desperately at the ropes that bound him. Behind the tree, Bowdrie could see the knot. He lifted the rifle and fired, heard the solid *thunk* of the bullet into the tree, and then, as he was cursing himself for his miss, he saw Venk spring away from the tree, fall, then roll into the shadows.

His bullet, aimed at the knot, had cut a strand of the rope!

The Apaches had believed themselves attacked by a number of men but would recover swiftly, realizing it could not be so. Warned by the fact that nobody had rushed the camp, they would be returning.

Bowdrie worked his way to where the horses were. He heard a sliding sound and a muffled gasp of pain.

"Venk?"

"Yeah." The whisper was so soft he scarcely heard it. "And I got my guns!"

A bullet smashed a tree near them, but neither wasted a shot in reply. They were thinking only of the horses now. The Apaches would think of them also. Suddenly Venk lifted his pistol and shot in the direction of the horses. Bowdrie swore, but the shot struck an Indian reaching for the rope that tied them. Startled by the firing, the horses broke free and charged in a body.

Bowdrie had an instant to slip his arm and shoulder through the sling on his rifle, and then the horses were on them.

He sprang at the nearest horse. One hand gripped the mane and a leg went over the back. Outside camp they let the horses run, a few wild shots missing them by a distance. They circled until they could come to where Bowdrie's horse was tied.

Daybreak found them miles away. Bowdrie glanced over at the big, powerfully muscled man lying on the ground near the gray horse. That it had once been a cavalry horse was obvious by the "US" stamped on the hip.

Naked to the waist, Venk's body was covered by burns. There was one livid burn across his jaw.

Venk looked over at him. "If anybody had told me that could be done, I'd have said he was a liar!"

Venk had two guns belted on, and in his wild escape from camp he had grabbed up either his own or an Indian's rifle.

"That was a tough one," Bowdrie admitted.

"You Rangers always go that far to take a prisoner?"

"Of course," Bowdrie said cheerfully, "I could have saved Texas a trial and a hanging or a long term in prison by just letting them have you."

"I guess," Venk suggested, "we'd better call it quits until we get back among folks. No use us fightin' out here."

Bowdrie shrugged. "What have we got to fight about? You're my prisoner."

"Determined cuss, aren't you?" He put a cigarette in his mouth. "Oh, well! Have it your own way!" He took a twig from the fire to light his smoke; then he said, holding the twig in his fingers, "I might as well go back with you. You saved my life. Anyway—" he grinned—"I'd like to stop by and see that Lucy gal! Say, wasn't she the—!"

He jumped and cried out as the twig burned down to his fingers, but as he jumped his hand dropped for his gun in a flashing draw!

The gun came up and Bowdrie shot him through the arm. Charlie Venk dropped his gun and sprang back, gripping his bloody arm. He stared unbelieving at Bowdrie.

"You beat me! You beat me!"

"I was all set for you, Charlie. I've used that trick myself."

"Why didn't you kill me? You could have."

"You said you wanted to see Lucy again. Well, so do I. I'd hate to have to go back and tell her I buried you out here, Charlie.

"Now, you just unbuckle that belt and I'll fix up that arm before you bleed to death. We've a long ride ahead of us."

About Louis L'Amour

"I think of myself in the oral tradition—as a troubadour, a village taleteller, the man in the shadows of the campfire. That's the way I'd like to be remembered—as a storyteller. A good storyteller."

It is doubtful that any author could be as at home in the world recreated in his novels as Louis Dearborn L'Amour. Not only could he physically fill the boots of the rugged characters he wrote about, but he literally "walked the land my characters walk." His personal experiences as well as his lifelong devotion to historical research combined to give Mr. L'Amour the unique knowledge and understanding of people, events, and the challenge of the American frontier that became the hallmarks of his popularity.

Of French-Irish descent, Mr. L'Amour could trace his own family in North America back to the early 1600s and follow their steady progression westward, "always on the frontier." As a boy growing up in Jamestown, North Dakota, he absorbed all he could about his family's frontier heritage, including the story of his great-grandfather who was scalped by Sioux warriors.

Spurred by an eager curiosity and desire to broaden his horizons, Mr. L'Amour left home at the age of fifteen and enjoyed a wide variety of jobs including seaman, lumberjack, elephant handler, skinner of dead cattle, assessment miner, and officer on tank destroyers during World War II. During his "yondering" days he also circled the world on a freighter, sailed a dhow on the Red Sea, was shipwrecked in the West Indies and stranded in the Mojave Desert. He won fifty-one of fifty-nine fights as a professional boxer and worked as a journalist and lecturer. He was a voracious reader and collector of rare books. His personal library contained 17,000 volumes.

Mr. L'Amour "wanted to write almost from the time I could talk." After developing a widespread following for his many frontier and adventure stories written for fiction magazines, Mr. L'Amour published his first full-length novel, *Hondo*, in the United States in 1953. Every one of his more than 100 books is in print; there are nearly 230 million copies of his books in print worldwide, making him one of the bestselling authors in modern literary history. His books have been translated into twenty languages, and more than forty-five of his novels and stories have been made into feature films and television movies.

His hardcover bestsellers include *The Lonesome Gods, The Walking Drum* (his twelfth-century historical novel) *Jubal Sackett, Last of the Breed,* and *The Haunted Mesa*. His memoir, *Education of a Wandering Man*, was a leading bestseller in 1989. Audio dramatizations and adaptations of many L'Amour stories are available on cassette tapes from Bantam Audio Publishing.

The recipient of many great honors and awards, in 1983 Mr. L'Amour became the first novelist ever to be awarded the National Gold Medal by the United States Congress in honor of his life's work. In 1984 he was also awarded the Medal of Freedom by President Reagan.

Louis L'Amour died on June 10, 1988. His wife, Kathy, and their two children, Beau and Angelique, carry the L'Amour tradition forward with new books written by the author during his lifetime to be published by Bantam well into the nineties—among them, three additional Hopalong Cassidy novels: *The Trail to Seven Pines, The Riders of High Ridge,* and *Trouble Shooter.*

LOUIS L'AMOUR

BANTAM'S #1
ALL-TIME BESTSELLING AUTHOR
AMERICA'S FAVORITE FRONTIER WRITER